CHRISTOPHER, RUNNING

ELISABETH PIKE

ISBN: 978-1-7385258-4-3

This paperback copy first published August 2025 by Little Bird Editions.

ABOUT THE AUTHOR

Elisabeth Pike is a freelance writer and maker. Her debut novel *Murmuration*, a YA dystopian survival story, was shortlisted for the Kindle Storyteller Award 2024. *Christopher, Running* is her second novel.

Find her at elisabethpike.co.uk

Christopher, Running
A novel

Elisabeth Pike

For my Uncle John

1

THE VILLAGE

 ugust 2013

'YOU STAY HERE, Es,' he says. 'They're coming for you.'

Christopher's hands are held out as if to steady her. Es is propped up against the hay bale, her eyes staring. Our hearts break as we watch from the rafters.

The shrill voice in his head is insistent and he babbles to try to silence it.

'No way this goes well,' he says, his fingers in his ears. 'They find her, they kill me. They don't find her; she'll be dead anyway. They'll never listen, they'll never forgive me.'

We can feel his brain racing, trying to work out all the ways that this could end. None of them are good. His eyes dart from place to place, wondering what to do.

We want to hold him in our ghost arms. Son of the village, our damaged boy.

The barn is a cloak around the pair of them, keeping

their secrets, but it can't stay this way. He knows he has to go.

A peel of corrugated iron curls up from the ground behind him - he had pulled it up earlier to squeeze in through the gap. He brought her here to keep her safe, hadn't he? To shelter her from the high August heat? Inside it is cool and dark, but his heart still races.

Now there are footsteps, and now there are voices, but the voice in his head shouts louder than them all.

'I have to go,' he says. 'They are coming. I have to go. You be safe now, little one.'

He takes one last look at her and then squeezes himself out into the day, the iron groaning as it bends back on itself.

Outside, the sun dazzles him, and he raises his arm to shield his eyes. He backs away from the search party. They are half a field away and the barn is between them, but he doesn't dare turn his back in case they set the dogs on him. He's always hated dogs.

There is a shout, and there is a bang on the door and then the crack of wood splintering as it's kicked down. He shudders. Our wretched bodies groan as we are pressed in to watch. 'He's so young,' we coo. 'So young, and he had the whole world in his hands.'

Christopher stumbles backwards and falls, his whole weight crashing awkwardly to the ground. He grabs handfuls of dry earth, fingernails clutching at the dirt, life of their own. Trying to bury himself or get him out of there. He is a cockroach scrabbling to get away, edging back from them across the furrows, his chest filling with a kind of sorrow and a thump of adrenaline. Rush of blood in his ears, breath heavy in his lungs.

We are the kiss of the slightest breeze on his face, the

rustle of crisp leaves on the hawthorn, we are the burning sun.

'What was I thinking?' he whispers, coming to a kind of clarity.

'Our little lost boy,' we croon, 'he's losing it all.'

His eyes dart from place to place, almost as if he has just woken up and seen this all for the first time. But his voice is not his own; it is outside of him, far away from him. He doesn't know what he has done, but he knows it is a bad thing. A wave of sickness rises from his toes through his chest cavity. He rolls over onto his hands and knees and retches.

'Can't stop here. Can never go back. Can never say sorry,' he whispers like a distant mantra. 'Can't stop here. Can never go back. Can never say sorry.'

He pushes himself up to standing and tries to run, but his legs are like wet mud. He can't get traction, can't push himself away from the ground fast enough.

But slowly he does it; he runs, crawls, pulls himself away from there.

Half a field away, he hides behind the hedgerow and looks back towards Alice. She is off in the far corner, small as a matchstick. A cluster of people, two cars. The sun beating down on them.

There are shouts from the barn.

'She's here!' someone calls.

'Thank God,' says another.

They stumble out again, waving their arms like air traffic controllers, carrying Esme across the field in their arms. The group of people start to run towards them.

Her mother, Alice, his only friend, snaps in two and drops to her knees.

Our village boy, what we would give to hold you. Alas,

we cannot, so we hide in the old oaks breathing husky sighs of relief.

Christopher watches like a creature in the hedgerow as they carry Es back across the field. He pushes himself low to the ground as Alice runs towards the search party. He makes himself so small. They carefully place Esme's body in Alice's arms, and she holds her tight against her chest. She rocks and lets out a howl. Her pain cracks the air like a gunshot, echoes around the razed field and bounces back from the sky.

Christopher cowers at the sound of her voice. Her grief gets into his bones.

From where he is lying, stomach flat to the hardened furrows, Alice looks different; her hair ragged and wiry, her body wracked with loss, already.

He turns and runs, giddy and nauseous; sick to death of himself.

Where he is going, he doesn't know, but he knows he must run because there is no other choice. 'How has it come to this?' he whispers, over and over. 'I loved her too, Alice. I loved her too.'

Then, he feels the whisper of the village and all of its raspy voices, like whispers in the wind, like papery autumn leaves, sliding against each other.

Us hawthorns twist and crack as he leaves our forcefield.

'How has it come to this?' we wonder, thinking back.

2

ALICE

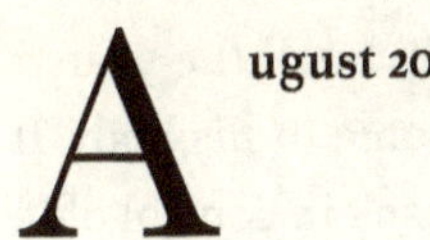ugust 2013

IN THE DAYS THAT FOLLOW, the rage burns in me.

All the paintings we made, and all the time that I gave him have gone up in smoke within me.

I am the smouldering wreck of that house he told me about, the one that the villagers burned to get rid of the outsiders, the ones they never wanted there in the first place. I am sodden with tears and only the ugly and charred timbers that hold me up still remain.

There is no love, no pity, no remorse. Only the anger that simmers, feeding on the childish love that I gave him for so long. I have wasted so many years.

I am so angry with myself that I didn't see him for what he was. How could I be so stupid? Fear torments me when I chase sleep. Why did I leave him so close to my daughter for so long? I lie awake, trying to imagine what he did to her, what he wanted with her, why he took her. I've asked myself so many times.

I've asked Esme over and over, but she won't speak.

Again, tonight, I whisper, 'You can tell me, Mummy won't be cross with you.'

But she just looks straight ahead, her elfin face pale in the light of the window.

'Did he hurt you?'

She shrugs, plays with her hands in her lap.

I know why she says nothing. She won't tell on him. He is her friend, and she loves him, still.

Christopher.

Sometimes I wonder if he was ever really in control, or if this thing was always bigger than himself. In all the years I have known him, he has never been at home in his body. It was as if it was too big for him, and he wasn't in control of it. He's a child inside a man's body; doesn't know his own strength.

See how I forgive him even now? I take the blame away from him, saying he was a child, it wasn't really him. Perhaps I'll always be making excuses for him.

He never wanted to grow up without Cassie, but he had to. His body dragged him through the years, and being pulled forward broke him, it tore him in two.

But if it wasn't really him that did this, then where is he, the man that I have shared my life with for the last eight years? Where has my Christopher gone? That gentle giant, carving birds for my girl, watching the swallows dart and loop over the fields with us?

The illness used to come and go, but it was never satisfied. It came for more and more of him, until, in the end, there was nothing left.

I try to picture him now, and I see him looking so scared;

scared of himself, scared of what he's done. I keep imagining the terror in his eyes, knowing that he's lost us; that he's done the most terrible thing.

I remember the day he came crashing into my life. Like a sharp cut, it sliced my life in two. I had just moved back up here after Ma died. I was washing up after dinner, looking out into the inky blackness. And then there he was, ghostly white in the dark, his face pressed up to the black windowpane.

'Shit!' I said, wiping the bubbles from my hands on the backs of my jeans.

'Christopher!' I said when I opened the door.

He stepped back.

'It's mother,' he said, panting, his cheeks red.

I hardly knew him. He had come to pay his respects at Ma's funeral as his mother was her friend. I'd seen him a little in the weeks that followed.

He looked away as if he was unsure whether what he was about to say was true or not. He fiddled with the hem of his red checked shirt and the laces from his work boots were hanging over the edges of his shoes. His jeans were dirty, and his hair was wild and unruly, his pupils dilated. I looked him over, disgusted and fascinated at once.

'I was at the pub,' he recounted breathlessly, 'I was whistling as I came around the corner of the house. I noticed there weren't no lights on. It was already getting dark. You see, normally she'd have tea on the go and the kitchen would be full of steam. I've run up through the horses' field to tell you just now, like.'

'Is she okay?' I asked.

'I shouted through the glass, but she didn't answer. She was lying across the table, her cake mix tipped up in front of her. She hadn't mixed in the margarine yet. I went in and touched her hand, but it was cold. Then I came to get you.'

'Did you ring for an ambulance?' I said, panicked.

He shook his head. 'No, I came to tell you!'

'Christopher! Shit!' I shouted, grabbing the phone in my soapy hands, and fumbling to dial the number.

We were too late; she'd been there all afternoon.

He didn't want to go home that night, so I made him up a bed in the lounge. He couldn't sleep though, so came and top and tailed next to me for warmth.

He was harmless, I thought.

There's a strange mixture of rage and pity when it comes to him. I don't know how to describe it, even now. Pity, already, after what he did. I'm molten with rage, but I'm also cracked in two. I know he won't survive on his own. However much I hate him, I don't want him to freeze to death in a ditch. No one deserves that. He is such an oaf, such a lump of life, that I can't imagine him making it to wherever he's trying to get to. I bet he doesn't even know where he's going. He must be reeling in shock at himself, and what he's capable of. He's probably scared shitless. What did he want with her? Where is he now? Will he ever come home?

I feel like his mother, his lover, his sister. And he, to me, is my family entire.

Paired atoms, around each other we spin.

Life fused us together. Neither of us willed it, it just happened, and now we're inseparable, whether we wanted it or not.

3

———

THE VILLAGE

July 1985

CHRISTOPHER AND CASSIE played on our roads as if they were playgrounds when they were young. They ran over our palms like feathers, they burned into the summer nights with their innocence. They roamed the place, treading it down into their skin and bone. We held them, watched them grow, safe as houses.

Slow-moving beacons in the delicious slip of time, they took each day as it came, each day as a gift, until it cut the cruellest trick, and snapped the stem of life, so young, so green. Precious young things they were back then, full of the hope of summer. They thought they had forever to play.

That one day, they ran their cars along our roads, pressing their cheeks to the gravel to line them up with precision. The imaginary crowds stilled to watch the races.

Cassie lay across from Chris on the grass verge, a flyaway

strand of her hair waving in the breeze, her face down to the ground to make sure there was a fair start.

The white pick-up truck set off quickly but then got caught in a pothole.

'False start!' complained Cassie. 'I wasn't ready!'

As the pick-up was trying to recover, the red sports car came up from behind and overtook it, but before it could reach the finishing line, the green car soared past them both like a bullet. Christopher held it tightly in his hand as he ran round in giddy circles. He became the driver of the car for a minute, letting out a cheer, then seamlessly, he became a plane flying over the stadium, and after that, he became a spectator, dancing on the verge. Cassie stood up with her hands folded in annoyance.

'Christopher, you always cheat.'

'Cass, I'm only messing. Let's have a re-run.'

They were crouched over the four cars, lining them up again, when they heard a rumble on the road surface. Christopher looked up to his left and saw a black car crawling past. They scrambled to their feet and looked up to see the driver shaking his head.

'You damn silly children,' the man shouted out of his car window. 'There'll be an accident someday!'

Christopher didn't meet the man's eyes but did his best to look sorry as the car passed. As soon as it disappeared around the corner, he stuck out his tongue and let out a cackle. Nobody could tell him what to do.

We loved those summer nights like they did; the ones that hung open, clear and quiet, waiting for strange happenings. The ones where the villagers were overcome by summer's madness, moving armchairs out onto the lawns to soak up each last drop of sun, drinking too much, Alfie kissing Rose behind the Five Bells, and then living to regret it afterwards. In the glare of the sunlight, the villagers felt they were famous, above reproach. Christopher and Cassie were touched by summer's madness too, made bold by its loving arms.

When the summer came, they could roam as they pleased. They walked the ditches and lanes together, rode their bikes through the village, along the sea bank to the Wash, where the sky was big, and the land eventually dissolved into salt water. They left their bikes in a heap at the gate and ran along the high banks of the Nene, past the twin lighthouses, where they stared out over the Wash, that half-way land of mud and sea. They lay back, heads on their rucksacks, and tried to spot patterns in the clouds.

They played in Christopher's overgrown garden; an entire world where sheds collapsed around their contents, chickens wandered freely, and the two of them tunnelled through overgrown thickets of brambles. They made dens in the ditch that ran alongside the garden, drew chalk pictures on the old outhouse wall. They gave the chickens rides in the wheelbarrow, made fairy gardens, climbed trees.

They hardly ate and their mothers never knew where they were but knew they would come in when they were hungry or cold.

They found Leo by accident. They were cutting across the Burns' farm one morning when Christopher stopped amidst a pile of junk, slowly realising there was an attempt at order around him. He saw the shears propped up against the glass, the deckchair set out rand the washing line hung from the hedgerow to the glasshouse frame.

'Someone lives here,' Christopher whispered.

'Nah,' said Cassie, 'come on.'

She looked around nervously.

Leo waited out of sight, listening. Christopher

approached the glasshouse and rubbed at the dirt with his jumper until he could see enough to peer in.

'Cass! I told you; someone lives here!'

Cassie was already turning away.

'Come on Christopher, we'll be late.'

Leo watched them walk away, and then the boy turned back, wondering.

He came by again that afternoon, dropped his school bag down in the long grass and pressed himself up against the glass panes to get a better view.

Leo came up behind him and placed a hand on Christopher's shoulder.

Christopher spun around and stared. The man's hair was white and wild, and his skin was as brown and wrinkled as a nut.

'I'm Leo,' he said, smiling.

Christopher's jaw hung open at the sight of Leo with his wiry hair and his mud-stained clothes.

'You're Joseph's boy, aren't you?' Leo asked. 'I picked with him on the farm.'

'Yes, don't tell him,' Christopher said, gazing up at Leo's stubbly jaw.

When Leo spoke, Christopher could see he was missing several teeth.

'Don't tell him what? That you were having a peek? It's a free country.'

Leo knelt to pull up some valerian that had sprung up around the door. He could feel the boy watching him.

'What's the matter with you?' he said, laughing. 'I don't bite!' He turned back to the weeding. 'Proper Fen man, your father.'

'Ain't you, then?' Christopher asked, in a quiet voice.

'Aren't I what?'

'A proper Fen man.'

'No, I don't like to think I am. I'm a man of the road.'

Leo pulled the door on its runner, where it now slid along happily.

'Why do you live out here?' Christopher whispered. 'You're like a field mouse or something, living in the hedgerow. Ain't you got a home to go to?'

Leo shook his head, shrugged.

'I've got all I need right here. Pitched up one day, asked Mr Burns if I could stop here and he didn't seem to mind.'

Christopher brought Cassie back with him that afternoon and over the course of that green summer, they learned all they could from Leo about the way that he lived. He taught them how to make a fire, how to cook a meal with one pan, how to camp out in the wild. Christopher was drawn to him, like a moth to a flame, fascinated that someone could live so lightly, without family, without things.

'I'M NOT ALLOWED to come anymore,' said Cassie, one day. 'My parents said they don't want me sneaking off all over the place.'

'Was that since they found out you were coming to see me?' Leo asked.

She nodded.

The rooks cackled on the wires in the silence that followed.

It felt like a tiny stab in his heart that his newest friend couldn't come any more.

'It's not your fault, darling, but I'm not so bad as they say, am I?'

She shook her head.

'No Leo, you're wonderful.'

She smiled at him with her mousy brown eyes.

He smiled and looked down, but the regret had already bitten him that day. He was drowning it the only way he knew how, and was already two bottles of red in.

'Are you alright, Leo?' Christopher asked.

Leo nodded and cradled a cup of wine between his hands.

Christopher and Cassie looked at each other.

Us dead ones knew that wine made everything softer. We knew it helped you to forget, to smudge away those memories that jagged you in the night. We knew that sleep was kinder than memory.

Cassie had her knees pulled up to her chest, her arms wrapped tightly around them, and Christopher played with strands of grass. They stayed with him because they didn't know what else to do.

'I'm not a bad man,' he said, rousing himself.

'They just don't know you, Leo,' said Cassie.

'I should never have done it,' he whispered, shaking his head.

'Done what?' Christopher asked.

'The bottle, I left it there,' Leo said. 'But it weren't for him.'

'For who?' Christopher said.

'It weren't for Jim. Wanted to finish George off, didn't I? After what he did to my brother.'

'You have a brother?' Christopher asked.

'Who's Jim?' Cassie asked, turning to Christopher.

And so, Leo told them. He couldn't help it; it spilled out of him, like tears.

'It was a burning day in June. Your father Joseph, Jim, and I were picking some strawbs,' he said, pointing to

Christopher. 'The sun was hot, and we'd been gulping down water by the bucketload. Our shirts were off our backs with the heat, as we bent and cut and bunched them all up. And on days like that, we always took our dinner break out there in the shade behind the tractor.

'And then I heard Jim spit out his mouthful, and I turned and see it like a bad dream. He was holding an unmarked bottle, and, thinking that it was water, and what with him being so thirsty with the work and the heat, he took a gulp.

'He spat half of it out right away, spluttering and red with the effort, but some had already gone down. I could see it stinging his insides; I could see it on his face. He was clutching at his neck. It was strychnine, the strongest rat poison we had.'

Christopher and Cassie looked at each other and could feel something breaking under them.

'I wanted to bat it out of his hand, but I froze. Then Joseph ran off and left me with Jim. I tried to make him sick, grabbing him up by his belly and trying to push it back up out of him but it was no use. It wouldn't come up again. I tried to pour water into his mouth, but it made him gag.

'So, I just stood there and watched him turn redder and redder. His eyes started to bulge out, and I didn't want to look at him, but I couldn't help myself. His face got all bloated and puffed out on the pillow of pale earth. His eyes were wide and panicky as he tried to get his breath. I started to panic too, shouting out his name. I dragged him over the furrows, his backside bumping along as I tried to get him to the road.

'"Jimmy! Anyone? Help!" I shouted. But I couldn't find no one about. I looked up the road one way and then the other, but I couldn't see nobody. There was just the heat rising from the road quivering up on the horizon.'

'Did he die?' Christopher whispered.

'He lay like a wounded fox at my feet, his head just about on my boot, and I was thinking about how I didn't want him to die with his head right there and then I saw Dr Giddings' black car on the road. I was waving frantically in the air, to show him where we were. He had Joseph with him, they came running across the field.'

'"I tried to make him sick, Doctor, but nothing came up," I told him. He slapped Jim's cheeks and pulled up his eyelids to shine his light into his pupils. Jim started to jerk then, and his eyes rolled back. "Joseph, you said he drank something?" the Doctor said, and Joseph ran over to get the bottle. Dr Giddings smelled it and said that it was strychnine for the rats, but what did he go ahead and drink it for?

'We shrugged and said we didn't know. But I knew.

'"Someone go and get his wife," said the doctor, and I nodded and started to run.

'He knew it was bad,' said Cassie, tentatively.

Leo nodded.

'Jessie came to the door all floury. "Making a pie," she said, holding her hands up, and then she looked at my face and said, "What is it?" wiping her hands on her apron. "It's Jim," I started to say, but she grabbed up the baby and pushed past me out of the door before I could say any more.

'"What's wrong?" she asked, running up the road in front of me, and I called, "Strychnine." That's all I needed to say; she knew it all right then. We ran all the way back to the farm. By the time we'd got there, Jim's back was arching up, his face twisted in pain. She knelt next to him, but his eyes were already cloudy.

'"What can you do for him, Doctor?" she asked, and he said, "I'm sorry, Jessie. There's nothing more I can do."

'"What do you mean? There must be something you can do! Has he had a drink? Surely, he can flush it out?"

'"I've tried to give him a drink, but he's convulsing too much to take it."

'"But why did he drink it?" she said, looking right at me.

'"It was an accident, an unmarked bottle," I shrugged. "Don't know what it was doing there," and the words of the lie melted into my shoulders and set my life off on a different course, right there and then. I've been lying since the day I saw him die.'

'It weren't your fault, Leo,' said Christopher, reaching out a hand to touch his knee.

'It were,' he said.

Christopher wondered why his father had never mentioned the poisoning, and he wondered what other secrets he was keeping.

Christopher and Cassie stayed with Leo until the light started falling, and then he leapt up saying, 'I'll walk you,' overprotective now, as he'd let his confession slip out into the world, and who knew where it would run. Tonight, it was a heavy load on their shoulders too, and Chris and Cassie walked topsy-turvy over the fields back to their homes under the weight of it. It would spread, Leo knew, but maybe it was time.

'Will you be alright, Leo?' Christopher asked, and they both turned to him, their faces like moons in the glow of the streetlight.

He nodded and turned away.

· · ·

THE NEXT MORNING, before Leo had even slept off his hangover, they were there again, banging on the glass.

Leo groaned.

He rolled over, pulled open the door and crawled out into the sunlight.

'We just wanted to check you were ok. After last night,' said Christopher.

Leo paused while it flooded back to him. He'd told them everything. He groaned.

'Ah, now,' he said, his heart already hammering inside his chest. 'I don't want you to be telling that story to anyone because people around here wouldn't understand. Is that okay? Do you follow me?'

They nodded.

'You haven't said anything already?'

They shook their heads.

'It's very important that no one knows,' he said, already knowing that the dam had been broken now, and the truth would trickle out in time. It had been held in for so long already; perhaps it was a good thing. He couldn't bear the weight of it any longer.

'Okay, good. How about I buy you two some chocolate to seal the deal?'

They looked at each other and grinned.

'Yes please!' they shouted at once.

'Alright, alright,' Leo said, feeling the dread of things shifting beyond his control. He knew this meant it was time for him to move on, which felt like a heavy grinding stone in his gut because he thought he'd found a home this time, he really did, and he was getting tired.

Us villagers could feel his discomfort. Would the road carry him once more? Would there be people to take him in? Could he ever shift the weight of this thing? If you take the life of a man and don't pay for it, can it ever be gone from you? If no one calls you guilty, then are you free? Everyone said it was an accident, but we'd known his secret for years. Now he cowered under the weight of it, tried to be as good as he could to pay it back. But nothing was enough.

Christopher and Cassie played leapfrog in the field while he dressed, then they ran down the road to the shop ahead of him, the soles of their shoes hitting the tarmac as they ran.

Things were already shifting like bruised clouds before a storm, and little did they all know that those precious few minutes were the very last time that everything was alright. They ran towards the end of everything without a care in the world.

4

THE VILLAGE

AFTERWARDS, it seemed that everything was broken, smashed to bits like clods of earth after the plough had passed over them. Christopher wasn't himself. How could he be without Cassie?

We saw him sitting in his back yard, alone, on a day towards the end of August. All of our arms wanted to pick him up and hold him, the little boy who had lost everything. The fair hair on his legs bristled in the breeze. We swirled around him, watching. The wind in our fingers picked up the leaves, scraping them across the dry ground. The earth was longing for rain.

His cat, Ginger, wound around him, her long body pressed against his back. She came and sat with him often these days.

A red tin bucket was set before him on the ground. He

stretched his fingers out behind him on the earth. He had been filling his bucket with debris from the back yard all afternoon: Tiny hard apples, stones, mud and dry leaves. Two tin soldiers. Brown leaves, curled over like the fortune-telling fish from crackers, were scattered around him. Two-faced, they were saying, as they lay there all twisted up. He packed the debris down with the back of his spade and the sharp points of his knuckles.

Christopher tipped the bucket over to turn out the sand-castle but there was nothing to hold it together and it crumbled and scattered. We picked up a few leaves and whisked them away.

It was only a few weeks ago that he had gone out to the Wash with Ben and Cassie. They pulled a kite across the embankment wall and the string scored into his hand. We watched as he pulled his hand up close to his face and looked at it. There it was – the faintest scar. It had really happened.

His mother had hidden his bike since, though, under a dust sheet in the shed. These days Christopher stayed close by.

A piece of chalk lay on the floor by the outhouse. Christopher wandered over, picked it up, then pulled string after string of ivy away from the outhouse wall. He stood back, looking at the wall for a moment. Then he drew a line for his height and started work. He sketched out the shape of a body; the same height as him. He drew the hair, eyes, blue shorts and a white shirt. Pigtails and yellow ribbons. There she was again.

'Christopher,' his mother whispered, behind him. She came up behind him and held his two shoulders with her hands.

Christopher threw the chalk on the ground and stared at the image he had made, biting his lip.

'It's her. We'll keep loving her, won't we? We'll never stop.'

Christopher nodded, biting back the tears.

'How can it be true? How can she not be here anymore?' we whispered on the wind.

'Do you think you could help me stir the jam?' his mother asked, nudging him with her elbow.

He shrugged and followed her into the kitchen where he washed his hands at the sink, pulled a stool up to the cooker and stirred the steaming pan of blackcurrants.

His mother handed him the bag of sugar.

'All of it?' he asked.

She nodded, and he poured it in and watched the deep red liquid seep up the side of the white sugar mountain.

'Are you okay?' his mother asked. 'You can talk if you want to, you know, any time.'

Christopher nodded and carried on stirring the jam.

She watched him for a while and then took the spoon and scraped some of the stuck sugar back down into the bubbling mixture at the bottom of the pan. She ruffled his hair with her hand and then he jumped down from the wooden stool and ran out of the back door again.

Christopher squeezed himself into the second shed between a rake and some planks just as the swollen sky let go of its first few drops of rain. It clattered down on the corrugated iron roof, immense and beautiful, and he stayed there, listening to it.

He wanted to be further in, between the planks of wood, with the spiders scratching. He squeezed himself along until he was pressed in on both sides, held up by the junk.

After a while, the rain softened. He rested his head on

the plank in front of him and listened. He heard his own heartbeat, a reminder of himself, the alive one. He stayed still, breathing slowly while his eyes adjusted to the light, straining his ears for any sound of life.

'Hello?' he whispered. The sound of his own voice was too loud, too close. He breathed in the smell of dusty wood.

'Cassie? Cassie?' he began, wondering if he could be so bold as to ask for her to come back.

And then, because the rain was thundering down again, he shouted at the top of his lungs, 'Cassie!' and he felt something crack; the barrier between them perhaps?

He stayed crunched up against the shed wall and listened to the rain. He waited for a long time. The rain felt like all the tears that he couldn't cry. They were shut up inside of him somewhere. He missed her so much he ached.

The rain eventually slowed, and he could hear his mother in the garden. She called out to him, but he was too tired and too sad to make his way to her. He heard a sigh and then there was nothing; just the sound of drips making their way in through the corroded corner of the shed. He looked down at the muddy rivulets running past his feet.

'If you come back, I'll never let anyone hurt you,' he whispered.

He waited for a long time. He waited until he felt calm again, and he waited until the rain had got through to him, penetrating all of his loneliness with its cold.

The rain lifted the smell of the fields and the roads as it always did until everything blended and became one smudgy waft of mud and road and hedgerow.

One of the planks had a nail sticking out at waist height and it caught on his red jumper as he pushed himself past it towards the door. He didn't care what his mother would say. He walked slowly back to the house.

When she saw him, his mother knelt at his level and started to cry. She put her face close to his and wrapped a towel around him. She felt along his arms and wondered how he stayed so dry while she was out looking for him. She was drenched through, her dark hair plastered to her neck, her dress clinging to her body.

She held him for a long time, his face getting clammy with the rain and heat.

'Oh, Christopher,' she said, as she put her arms around his skinny shoulders. 'I don't know what to do with you.'

She didn't say anything about the pull in his jumper but peeled off his damp jeans and fetched him some clean clothes from upstairs. She made a fire even though it was the middle of the day. She told him to sit down and wait while she made him a cup of tea. Christopher was too tired to protest. He just sat there, letting his mother's love wrap around him like a blanket.

That day with the jam was the first time that he talked to Cassie, but it carried on in the coming weeks as he filled and refilled his bucket with dirt, and as he wandered slowly under the trees and through the long grass of his parents' home. If his mother had looked out to watch him playing in the back yard, she might have seen his lips moving to themselves. He sometimes started laughing to himself. It made him feel normal again. It was only at night when he crawled into the heavy double bed that he shared with his brother that he had to imagine the words that he wanted to say to her. He knew that Ben wouldn't understand.

'Goodnight Cassie,' he would mouth into the dark room, his tongue clicking against his teeth.

Life carried on, inexplicably.

When he first started going back to see Leo, it felt painful. How could they sit there in the sunlight, pulling up the grass, listening to the birds, feeling the wind on their faces, without Cassie? They sometimes didn't know what to say to each other anymore, and that just made everything worse, so Christopher started to avoid him. They never got back the easy friendship they'd had that summer. Too much had been lost between them.

After a month, Christopher's parents were happy with him working up the farm on a Saturday with Ben. It was strawberry season and there was always work to be done. They thought it might burn up some of his anxiety. To start with, people were kind but, as time went by, they began to get agitated when they talked to him.

'Are you listening to me?' they'd say, but Christopher was hardly there anymore. He felt that nothing mattered, not the words they were saying or even eating or breathing. He'd gone to a place beyond them all. A place where he could still talk to her.

Our lost boy.

'You can't keep talking into thin air, Christopher,' Ben said, shaking his head. 'You're in a dream world. There's real life going on here, and you're missing it.'

Christopher looked down and began to furiously pull strawberries off the plants, uprooting them when the fruit didn't come away easily. Ben didn't understand. He had never even tried.

Because there was so much fruit that year, the other villagers had been pulled in to help. Even Mrs. Burns was working that day. The air was heavy with the scent of the fruit. Mrs Burns looked up at Christopher and pulled down the corners of her mouth as Ben walked away.

'You've upset him there,' she said with a smile.

Christopher looked at her and his fringe fell into his eyes. He moved it aside with a soil-covered hand, leaving a faint smear across his forehead. They watched Ben march off in his heavy black boots, churning up bits of soil as he went.

She turned to Christopher and said in a whisper, 'Don't you worry. I used to talk to Edmund all the time, my boy that went missing. I know what it's like to talk to someone who ain't here anymore.'

Christopher nodded vaguely. 'Edmund. I heard about him.'

Another one of our lost sons, he set fire to a house for fear of his father. Even now, no one really knows what happened except for us. We felt the fear burn in his heart; we saw him running with no rest. He'd backed himself into a corner, dear boy, and it was the only way he could think to get away.

Christopher turned back to the row, feeling for the bright clusters of fruit more gently now.

'Missing,' he said to himself, 'maybe she's just gone missing.'

5

—————

THE VILLAGE

September 1990

WHAT COULD we do for Christopher, as old as we were? What could we do but hold him with our shushing willow, our empty skies, our icy winds? There was no way we could give back what had been taken.

In the end, he had to learn to grow lopsided, a wind-blasted hawthorn.

And then the day came when it was time for Ben to leave the village and move on to college. We saw him moving around the bedroom, picking things up and setting them down again.

And later, just as Ben was about to board the bus, he turned to see Christopher run down the road.

'I thought you weren't coming,' Ben said.

'Course I was,' Christopher said, heaving, dizzy from the

bus fumes. 'Come back soon,' he mumbled. 'I'll miss you, Ben.'

'I'll try. I'll see you soon.'

Their father held out a hand to shake Ben's.

'Good luck, son. Come back, won't you?'

Ben nodded.

'Don't know why you young folk have to leave. I've never needed anything outside of this place.'

Ben looked at him, surprised by what his father really thought. He'd never said before. They shook hands, and Ben took the formality as a slight. Ben kissed his mother goodbye and then turned away.

They watched as he struggled to get his bag through the doorway of the bus. They waved as the bus pulled away but were quickly engulfed in a cloud of fumes.

Their parents walked slowly back down the driveway.

'I must get on with that bonfire; I've been meaning to do it for ages,' Joseph muttered, and he wandered down the garden, whistling as he went. On to the next thing.

Marjorie took a few steps and then faltered.

'What now?' she said.

Chris didn't know where to go except for the willow on the front lawn. He entered its cool sanctuary of leaves with the yellow-dappled light filtering through and sat there with his back pressed against its rough trunk. He stayed there for what seemed like hours until, finally, the tears came.

They came for Ben, for his family, for Cassie, for all that was changing under his feet and all that he couldn't hold on to. Life was falling through his hands, and he couldn't get a grasp on it.

We knew how he felt for we felt it too. Nothing stayed the same.

6

————

THE VILLAGE

November 1993

CHRISTOPHER RESENTED GROWING UP AFTERWARDS. He dug his heels in, but time kept ticking on. He still went to see Leo every now and then, but the fissure had grown and was painful, and Christopher was lopsided, one half of a pair. Their friendship faded until there was barely a nod between them as they passed on the road.

AND THEN, one day, worn down by the weight of the past, Leo lay down in his beloved glass house and let it become his tomb. He looked through the lichen-encrusted panes at the blue sky and drank the clear tasteless poison that he knew would slow his heart and stop up his blood. It was the same poison he laid out as a trap for his boss, the boss who he believed had chased Leo's own brother from the land

and burned his home to the ground, who made it look like an accident, who thought that nobody knew.

We swaying trees knew that that was why Leo had come in the first place; for his brother, because the anger didn't fade over the years like he thought it might. That's why he tried to kill him. To pay back the pain of his brother's family, who had to watch their home burn to the ground, who had to run away from here with nothing, absolutely nothing to their name.

But he never meant for Jim to drink it. He didn't mean to rob Jessie of her life with him. Oh, how he wished he could go back and change things. But life was too cruel for that. And so, in taking his life, he paid back his debt so he could die with no burdens.

Leo didn't move on to another place like he thought he might, even after he told the children and spilled his secret out into the world because, right afterwards, the world ended again, in another way. Jim and then Cassie. His fault again.

He could never find a way to make things right again. He could never find the words to say sorry to Christopher. They both knew there was no way to make anything better. They still talked from time to time, but Christopher's whole body was shattered, and Leo didn't know how to hold it.

And then one day in June, he woke, and he knew it was time.

After he swallowed the poison, he could feel it stinging his insides, and he hoped that nature wouldn't mind that he'd cheated his way out of life.

His eyelids fell shut and he slipped into oblivion, memory, folklore.

When the villagers found his cold, grey body, days later, and the note, written in his own hand – just two words: 'I'm sorry' – they tucked him into his beloved earth with no malice, not knowing or really minding what he did.

But he knew. And in his last act, dear Leo tried to make things right again, the only way he could, with the only thing he had left to give – his life.

Cassie didn't get the chance to breathe a word of his secret, and Christopher knew not to for loyalty, and it was not until years later, when there was someone who needed to know, that it all flooded back to him.

And over the years, as the worms made their home in Leo's body, taking back what once was theirs, and as the hawthorns pushed their spiny roots into his lung cavities, he became them, and they learned from him.

Once homeless, in his dying, he became one with us, the village; became its very lifeblood. He lay down with all of us who had gone before him. He took on our secrets and shame, our hard-won wisdom and dogged determination. He took on all of our understanding, all of our seeing. Our voices in the hedgerows gave him life again, as he rose in sap to the very tips of our branches. He joined us to watch Christopher, the twisted hawthorn, as he tried, or should we say failed, to make sense of his life without her.

7

———

THE VILLAGE

J une 1999

CHRISTOPHER DIDN'T GO FAR when he was grown, just to the bottom of his parents' garden to an old static caravan. He had nowhere else to go did he? Thought the world was so small, that the village was all that mattered. He was still searching, after all, and this was the only place she'd be.

We held him at the hardest times, like when he lost Leo, and then, years later, in a warm June, when he was 21, and the urgent knocking on the caravan door woke him, and his mother called 'Chris! Are you awake? It's your father.'

She wrung her hands together, her breath circling away from her in the morning chill.

Christopher opened the door; his face still creased from sleep.

'He's gone, Chris.'

Christopher said nothing as he followed his mother

back through the garden to the house, ran straight up the stairs and sat on the bed next to his father. He tried to pull his body up by the shoulders, saying, 'Dad, Dad, it's morning!'

'Chris don't!' Marjorie called, and she put her arms around her son to pull him away.

'He's asleep Mum, that's all, I know it.'

'No, Chris, he's not!'

They stumbled back into the wardrobe, which clunked backwards against the wall.

'Dad! Dad! Wake up or they'll think you're dead!'

'He's gone, love.'

After that, Christopher sat on the edge of the bed and prodded his father's cheeks with a finger. He touched his hair. He held his hand.

'Are you sure you're dead, Dad?'

Then, when there was no reply, he turned to his mum and said, 'Are you sure he's dead?'

She nodded.

For the rest of that day, Christopher tiptoed around his mother. She sat there quiet and pale in Joseph's chair, drinking tea. She telephoned Ben at breakfast time, and he said he'd come as soon as he could.

After that, they let the telephone ring between them like a siren. Word would get around, it always did.

At six o'clock, after asking her three times if she was okay, Christopher went out walking. He felt the pull of his footsteps towards the door of the Five Bells before he had even stepped out of his mother's door.

'You sure you'll be alright?' he called, not looking back.

· · ·

LATER ON THAT NIGHT, Christopher sat on the steps of his caravan smoking a rollie. He was thinking about the way his dad said he never needed to leave the village, and about how Leo had never been able to stay anywhere. He was thinking about Cass, how she wandered off and never came home. Funny how different folks can be. All these ones moving on and he'd not got Cass back yet.

The kitchen light flicked on, and he could see his mother moving around the kitchen in her nightdress. She poured herself a glass of water and then opened the back door and walked out into the June night. She walked slowly around the garden, put one hand against the shed and looked up at the stars.

Christopher's roll-up glowed in the night.

He didn't want to startle her, so he called quietly to her, 'Mum, I'm over here.'

'Oh, hello, love,' she said, not really looking at him.

She didn't seem surprised to see him sitting there, but walked towards him, past the shed, which was slowly collapsing under its own weight. It seemed to hold the undoing gently, this garden. It was allowing itself to disintegrate, for it knew that was the natural order of things.

'What are you doing out here?'

'Couldn't sleep.'

'Neither could I.'

The summer night was close around them. She wandered over to the swing and rocked back and forth in the night, a ghost in her nightdress.

CHRISTOPHER DIDN'T KNOW how to behave at his father's funeral. After the service, he slipped away, not staying for the food but wandering across the fields instead.

The telegraph poles were giants holding up the wires, striding across the flat fields.

Ben found him later when the heat had gone from the day. He was sitting by the side of the road, smoking a cigarette.

'You know I knew when it happened,' Ben said, the beer loosening his tongue.

Chris looked up at him with a puzzled expression.

He sat down next to Christopher.

'Lend me a ciggie will you?'

'Didn't know you smoked,' said Christopher.

'I don't. It woke me up, the thought that something had happened.'

Ben looked at Christopher.

'I sat up in my bed, I said "What was that?" to Anna. She said it was nothing and told me to go back to sleep, but I got up, walked around the house, checked the doors and windows, checked the children. Everything was fine. I lay back down and tried to sleep but I knew something was wrong. And then in the morning, Mum was on the phone saying he'd died in the night.'

'Maybe it was his way of saying goodbye,' Christopher said, matter-of-factly.

Ben took a drag on his cigarette and sighed.

'So, you believe in ghosts then?'

'He just had to tell you he was going,' Christopher shrugged. 'He didn't tell me.'

'Little brother, why is everything so easy for you to believe?'

'It happened, didn't it? You woke in the night?'

Ben nodded, 'Yes, but ...'

His thought trail faded away to nothing and they sat there together as the light fell away.

'You ain't coming home are you, Ben?'

He shook his head.

'I'm happy in the hills, with Anna and the kids. It feels like home there too now.'

IT WAS a few months after the funeral and Marjorie was dusting. Ben, Anna and the children were coming for the weekend again. She had opened the front door, which was rarely opened, to give the dust somewhere to go. There was a sweet smell from apples that had fallen all around the doorway and been trodden into the grass.

Marjorie shook the net curtains outside the door and dust particles sailed across the room, lit by the sunlight that came streaming in.

Christopher was at the house more these days. He didn't know where else to go, and he knew that his mother needed him. Now his father was gone, Marjorie was going to see about selling the smallholding, it was too much for Christopher to take on. Christopher still worked the odd day at the Burns' farm and that was enough. He would turn up in the morning and if there was anything, they'd keep him. It suited Christopher.

Steam from the kettle filled the kitchen and Christopher assembled teabags, milk and mugs, before taking two of the dining room chairs out into the garden.

They sat down together with their mugs of tea and let the sunshine warm their skin.

'You going up the farm today, then?' Marjorie asked.

Christopher shaded his eyes with his hand and looked over at his mother, her head resting against the back of the chair, her eyes closed, her mug of tea held close to her chest.

'I'll go up later. Thought I'd stay here for a bit first.'

'Christopher, you know I'll be fine, don't you? I can manage on my own.'

He nodded.

'Mum, I don't know if I like it up the farm anymore.'

'Did something happen, love? Up there?'

'I was late again. He shouted at me.'

'Those bloody Burns, they're all as bad as each other. You have got to be on time though, love. Shall I try knocking for you again in the morning, like I used to? Maybe that'll work?'

'Maybe.' Christopher paused for a moment. 'Mum?'

'Yes, love?'

'Where's Dad? I haven't seen him for days.'

She sat up and looked at him and then sighed, not knowing where to begin.

'Have you two had a fight?'

Her voice came out wobbly when she said, 'He's dead, pet, don't you remember?'

Christopher's hand went up to his face, tracing the shape of his lips with his finger.

Marjorie watched him trying to piece it together.

'Oh, oh, that's right, I forgot. I forget sometimes,' he answered, his eyes crunched up in the September sunlight. 'Forget what's real.'

'I'll sort through his things,' Marjorie said, 'it'll be easier for you that way.'

Later on that morning, when Ben, Anna and the children pulled up in the driveway, Christopher was sketching the outline of a face onto the wall of the outhouse. When he had finished, he turned and looked over his shoulder to Sam.

'Come and have a go, Sam,' Christopher called. 'Keep

your eye on the target, bring your arm up over your head and release it just when your arm gets to here,' he said.

Sam watched carefully and laughed when his uncle missed the target. He tried to copy, picking up a rotten apple and launching it as hard as he could. It just missed the face. Sam delighted in the smack as the apple hit the brick.

Ben embraced his mother and they watched from the back door.

'How is he? How are you?' said Ben.

'Taking each day at a time.'

His father had been like a paperweight in Christopher's life, weighing him down, pinning him to the earth. And now that he was gone, Christopher was scattered to the wind. Like before, with Cassie.

But we watched as he tried to find reasons to live; the cups of tea with his mother, the birds with broken wings that he would try to nurse back to health. It was the littlest things. It was the same for his mother. The strawberries were good that year and she made jam obsessively.

For Christopher, though, the smell of the jam, sickly sweet, took him back to that other summer, the one when everything changed.

Ben and Marjorie watched from the doorway, and Anna came to join them.

'Do you think he's getting worse?' Ben asked in a quiet voice.

'Yes,' whispered Marjorie. 'I can't keep track of him, and I don't think he's safe on his own. He's still that seven-year-old boy who lost everything. He's forever out playing.'

'The children are like medicine to him,' Anna whispered. 'Maybe he just needs more people around him.'

'I don't know what he needs,' said Marjorie. 'I feel like he's lost his grip on things, somehow.'

Christopher, who could hear every word they were saying, knew what he needed, and we knew it too. It was to find Cassie, to have his father back, to have his old self again.

LATER ON, when Christopher still hadn't arrived for dinner, and the others had given up waiting and started without him, he ran into the living room, carrying something wrapped in sacking.

'It's Whitey,' he said.

His eyes darted from face to face, not knowing where to look.

Ben pushed back his chair and stood. His children were staring open-mouthed at Christopher.

'Let's go outside,' Ben said, and he led his brother out by the arm. 'It's not Whitey, Chris, it's Tinker, remember? Whitey died a long time ago.'

'Oh yes, yes.'

Chris put the bundle on the kitchen floor and unwrapped his hoodie to look at the cat's body.

He sobbed like a baby.

After a while, Ben spoke.

'Shall we bury her after dinner?' he asked. 'Come and eat with us.'

'I can't leave her,' Christopher sobbed. 'You go. I'll stay here.'

After dinner, they walked to the end of the garden, where it narrowed. There was a path to the right between a shed and the compost heap. Christopher walked along it until he reached the hedgerow and began to dig. He dug angrily, holding the spade high and crashing it down onto the soil, flinging the mud over his shoulder.

'It's okay, Chris,' Ben said, reaching out to touch his arm.

Christopher snatched his arm away from him.

'It's not okay,' he shouted, through tears, 'everything dies!'

They laid the bundle in the bottom of the pit and started to cover her back over when Lucie came running outside.

'Daddy, are you coming back in?'

'Yes, love, give me five minutes.'

'Okay.'

Lucie didn't move but stood twisting her hands together, watching the soil being flung into the hole.

'Is it the cat, Daddy?' Lucie asked. 'What happened?'

'It was probably hit by a car, darling.'

'Oh,' she said, peering into the makeshift grave.

Christopher threw down his spade and walked away, leaving Ben to answer his daughter's questions.

As Christopher was pacing up and down in the garden, not knowing what to do with his anger, he heard Sam's voice from under the willow tree.

He listened as his nephew chatted away to himself and his racing heart began to slow. He wiped his eyes and pulled back the branches.

'Are you okay, Uncle Christopher?' Sam asked, stuffing something quickly into his pocket.

Christopher stepped inside the willow's embrace and sat down next to Sam.

'No,' said Christopher. But then, after a pause, he added, 'When I was little, I used to have a friend that I talked to like you do. My friend was called Cassie. What's yours called?'

Sam looked at him shyly.

'He's called Goblin,' Sam said, as he pulled a squishy ball with a face out of his pocket.

'Well, Goblin, it's very nice to meet you.'

Sam looked at him for a moment and then said, 'You're not like other grown-ups, are you?'

Christopher laughed. 'Suppose not.'

Sam nodded, and then asked, 'Where's Cassie now?'

'She went off wandering,' said Christopher, pointing down to the bottom of the garden. 'I'm still trying to find her.'

Sam looked at him for a while, and then said, 'Well, where have you looked for her?'

Christopher shrugged, 'Everywhere I can think of.'

'Don't give up,' Sam said, his earnest little face peering up at Christopher.

Sam jumped to his feet and ran out from under the willow before Christopher could think of a way to reply.

The curtain of leaves fell back into place, hiding him from sight almost completely.

8

ALICE

 pril 2005

'BUT PETE, we keep going around and around in circles!' I say, slamming my hand down on the table. 'You know why I need the summer on my own. I have to get this collection finished. It's more important than anything.'

'More important than me?'

'Yes. Right now, my work is my priority.'

He looks at me with red-rimmed eyes and reaches over to try to take my hand, but he's already had too much lager and he's just saying the things I want to hear.

'Babe, we can work it out ...' he begins, but I can't cope with it anymore and I stand up, snatch my ridiculous glittery handbag from the table, and walk out into the night.

Of course, he follows me, running up the road behind me as I march along in my heels.

'Pete,' I say, and as I do I think to myself, I don't want to end things, do I? God knows. But I'm so frustrated. 'I need to be on my own. I think we should take a break. I can't do this anymore.'

His face falls and he stops following me. I can't bear to look at him, so I keep walking.

I WAKE THE NEXT MORNING, hungover.

'Urgh,' I moan.

I sigh and reach up to rub my eyes. The alarm is screeching. 6 am. It is my turn to open up at the cafe.

In the shower, I let the water wash away the regret of the night before.

I feel sick. I was childish, as always, I didn't talk things through, I just said my piece and walked away, but I still think it's the right thing to do. He's so over the top that I feel suffocated. There. I've said it. There's no other way I can put it. And even though I feel crushed by the thought of his anger, it still feels like it is the right thing. Every conversation, he brings around to his way again. Every decision, he twists backwards. It feels too hard to stretch my legs out, to breathe with him around. And I know I'm too old to be breaking up with men who aren't that bad, but at the same time, he makes my skin crawl.

'I'm probably never going to have kids,' I whisper into the hot shower water, and I feel numb with it, but no kids is better than kids with the wrong man, surely?

There was nothing I could have changed, was there? Probably. Probably could have done the whole damn thing differently. But I need to breathe. By myself for a while. I need to remember how to think straight. I know he'll call me today. I know he won't let me go.

I turn off the water, dry myself and get dressed for the

day. I tie my hair up with a red scrunchie and throw on black flares and a bright red t-shirt. Dress bright to lift my mood.

No time to eat, I'll graze later at the cafe.

As I walk across the city, I can hear the slow beeps of the recycling lorries, gathering early morning rubbish. I have always found the noise strangely comforting; safe, somehow. I guess it's the sound of people living. I've always liked the cool morning air, the quietness of the street, the secrets of the morning. Even with a low-level headache. I breathe in the new day and wonder what it will bring.

The cafe is in this tiny courtyard which has the best smells. It is tucked under the wing of a hotel, so the smell of fresh laundry drifts down into the courtyard, and there is a florist opposite, so the fresh green scent of life and blooms washes over too, and, of course, it's all mixed with the scent of freshly ground coffee.

I haul open the metal shutter halfway and duck underneath. Out back, I put the radio on loud, swig water to dilute the hangover and start the stew of the day. I chop onions, courgettes, red peppers, aubergines, and fresh tomatoes. I throw them all in a pan to simmer down with garlic, salt, and olive oil. The smell makes my stomach rumble and I remember that I still haven't eaten.

What could be so life-affirming as food, I wonder. What could be better than a job that literally feeds people?

I have five minutes to spare, so I grab a muffin from the counter and eat it before getting out a frozen tray of muffins and a lemon loaf cake. I make up some paninis for the day: hummus and roasted vegetables, pesto and mozzarella cheese, pastrami and pickles.

I look at the clock. 7.30 am.

Time to clean the loo, top up on napkins, get the tables out in the courtyard and unlock the front door.

Soph arrives at 8.00 am, ready for the regulars. There's a few who stroll in a few minutes later, for a coffee on the way to work, the couples that pop in for breakfast every now and then, the mums who come after the school run with one less child. All of them looking for caffeine. Always the caffeine. There are the ones who order the same thing every time, like Bernie, who comes in for his pot of tea at midday, or the couple who always take the same table outside.

'Two grande lattes,' she says in her Italian accent.

It's Sophie's cafe not mine, but I share the load. We live together and run the cafe together. We are a warm place on a cold day and refreshment in the sunshine. It sometimes feels like we are offering a hug to anyone who needs it. Sometimes it feels as if all the world's troubles are held outside of our caffeine-fuelled bubble of welcome, cinnamon and Earl Grey. It feels like we could fix everything right here.

I realise halfway through the morning that I haven't even told her about Pete yet.

Soph lets me go a little early since I opened up. Later, I can hear the telephone ringing as I am unlocking the door to the apartment. It is 3.15 pm. I drop my bags just in time to get to the phone.

'Hello?'

'Love?'

'Ma? Are you okay?'

She sounds far away.

'I've had a fall. I don't want you to worry, but do you think you could come?'

I sigh.

'Of course.'

It takes me nearly two hours to make the journey from Cambridge and all the way there I think about the last time I went up, and we had that row, and I left in a rage, my eyes filled with tears, and shouted at myself in the car because she was just an old woman, my mother, and she had nothing left but me. But she drove me crazy. I was never enough for her, and she was always at pains to remind me of it, in all the ways she could. That's why I hardly went back.

When I get there, she is alone, sitting up at the table leaning all her weight on it, her right arm held close to her ribs. She looks uncomfortable but smiles as I let myself in with my key.

'Nice to see you, love,' she says, trying to turn, but wincing.

'Oh, Ma. Can you move your arm at all?' I ask.

She tries and sucks in sharply.

'Let's get you to the hospital.'

'I don't know, Alice. I was thinking you could just have a look; you'll know all about it. I'd rather not go to hospital.'

'Ma, you can't even move it, you've broken your collar-bone or something. Have you had any painkillers?'

'No, love, nothing.'

I find a packet of paracetamol and run her a glass of cool water from the tap, which she gulps down.

'Have you had anything to eat?'

She shakes her head.

I make her a sandwich, thinking this is all a ruse to get me to feel guilty. Isn't it, Ma? You knew I couldn't be here for you, which is why you called me. She eats, quietly. I pack a few bits for her, thinking the hospital might want to keep her in overnight.

I lift her good arm and put it around my waist, while she holds the other arm tightly to herself and tries to stand.

'Why didn't you call Marjorie?' I say, the frustration getting the better of me.

'I wanted you to sort me out.'

'But Ma ... I'm so far away ... She's just down the road ...'

I trail off.

'You should have called someone.'

SHE MANAGES to shuffle to the car, wincing and pursing her lips with each step. Her scarlet slippers make a scratching noise as they move across the surface of the path, dragging bits of gravel along with them.

At the hospital, after hours of waiting in corridors, the doctor tells us that she has fractured two ribs. Tears pinch at the corners of my eyes. Guilt pinches my gut.

'We'll keep her in overnight, just as a precaution,' says the doctor. 'You can stay as long as you like tonight.'

'She's a doctor,' Ma says, pointing at me.

I shake my head at the doctor.

'No, I'm not,' I say, embarrassed. 'I used to be a nurse.'

The doctor smiles tightly.

'Ma, you should have called an ambulance. I had no idea it was this bad.'

'Ring the buzzer if you need anything,' the doctor says, eager to get away from our quarrel, and she squeaks away down the corridor in her rubber-soled shoes.

The ward falls quiet aside from bleeps and occasional footsteps. I look around at the other beds, curtained off from each other. I fuss over her, asking if she wants water or tea, but she lies back and closes her eyes.

'What did you mean when you said, used to be a nurse?'

I was hoping she hadn't noticed.

'I'm just taking a break for a little while. Working with Soph at the cafe.'

She opens her eyes and looks at me with that mixture of compassion and pity that I can't stand.

'Oh, Al.'

Condescending even when lying on a hospital bed.

'Get some rest, Ma. I'll stay here. We can talk tomorrow.'

I sit there in the dark next to her. I'd not been in a hospital since I quit nursing. I'd not seen Ma either. Couldn't hack it.

I used to work in oncology. There was a little boy called Sammy that I practised my platitudes on. When they didn't work, and when he died, I decided I couldn't do it anymore. I couldn't lie to any more kids. I couldn't tell them that they'd be okay. I couldn't use that sing-song voice if I couldn't fix them. Even now, the anxiety was rising, and the clinical smell was making me feel sick to the stomach. It was just too much.

The cafe feels better, though. We are meeting simpler needs. Hunger. Thirst. Loneliness. We can fix those things.

I leave Ma sleeping and wander out into the corridor to call Sophie.

'I just wanted to let you know where I was,' I whisper.

'What time is it? I assumed you were with Pete.'

I look over at the clock. It is after midnight.

'Sorry,' I say, rubbing at my forehead with my palm, 'I didn't realise how late it was. My mum's had a fall, so I had to come up. She's cracked two ribs, so I'll have to stay for a while. I won't be able to work my shifts for the next few days, I'm sorry.'

I hear a sigh.

'I'm sorry babe' I say.

'Don't be silly, you have to be with Jessie. I'll figure it out.'

'I'll call you. Oh, and babe, I broke up with Pete.'

'What?'

'Long story. Tell you soon.'

'Okay. Bye, hon.'

I feel bad leaving her in the lurch with the café, but what can I do? I wander down the hallway looking for a cup of tea, but the cafes are all shut. There is a vending machine in the hallway, and I punch in the number for white tea, one sugar, then carry it back to her bedside, sipping the scalding tea at intervals and waiting for morning.

They kick me out after breakfast.

I go back to her house. The house I grew up in. I'm hoping for a shower and some rest. But first, I walk around slowly, taking in the quiet, the feel of the place. I haven't been here alone for a long time. I feel like a trespasser, imagining her eyes watching me as I stand in the spaces that I grew up in.

There are countless packets of food stacked up neatly in the pantry, tins of beans and meats; more than she could ever eat.

Upstairs, I find a box of letters from me on the desk in the bedroom. I read some of them back and am surprised how quickly the years have gone by, and how the intention to come back to visit faded more and more each year. Reading them back, it just feels like excuse after excuse. How could I have been so selfish?

After Dad's accident, she dug her heels in and made a life for herself here. She had her friends, her chores, her ways.

We took in Leo, a farmer, over one of the harshest winters. He lived in a glasshouse over on the Burns' farm. Just pitched up one day looking for work by all accounts. He only stayed until the thaw – didn't like to depend on anyone

– but I still remember the day he moved in. I opened the door and showed him around as if it was all mine. I was so cocky then; full of life and confidence.

I wonder what happened to that girl as I notice that the wallpaper I chose for my bedroom is still there, fading on the walls. The wooden bed frame is still painted pink. Leo helped me to do that for my seventh birthday. We tipped the mattress up on its end and left it leaning against the wall while we covered the floor in newspaper and opened the windows wide. She must have kept it in case I ever had children.

It is disorienting to be back, and for Ma not to be there. I can't visit again until two o'clock, so I lie down on my childhood bed and stare up at the ceiling.

I wake, later, confused, with a headache and a dry mouth. It's 5.15 pm. I've missed the afternoon visiting hours, so I call the ward and say I'll be there in the morning.

The house speaks to me in the silence.

There are so many memories here, so much happiness and confusion. So much frustration. Ma wanting to be everything for me when she knew she couldn't be. Ma wanting me to be everything that she thought was best. So, then, I just ran. Soon as I could. I couldn't stand it anymore. I knew I couldn't be what she wanted so I kept running. Only came back briefly, talking all the time, pretending to be happy, just so I had a reason to not be here. Used the noise of my life to cover everything over.

But now I'm stripped of Pete, of work, of all the other things that kept me away. Never heard the house so quiet as it is now. Don't want to give it a chance to talk to me, but I can't help myself. This place has its claws in me.

'Here I am,' I whisper into the damp and quiet room, despite myself. 'I'm back.'

. . .

THE NEXT MORNING, I make strong black coffee and stand barefooted on the cold quarry tiles in the lounge of my childhood. Two armchairs are pulled up to the fire, and it feels as if my five-year-old self will come running in from the garden at any moment with an armful of eggs, asking to make a cake or for a drink of hot milk. I'd love to see her again, my younger self. I'd love to tell her that she will be ok, that she doesn't need to worry about growing up without a dad and that she will manage it somehow.

I walk a lot and it feels like coming up for air. I have been so busy running the café with Soph that I've not had much time to think. It feels good to stop, to be away from Cambridge. To be away from Pete.

We just sort of fell together. We both knew we were too old to be coasting, and it was time to start settling down, which added a certain pressure. Neither of us were very sure about it. Or at least I wasn't. He had this way of talking me into things, and it was hard to think straight around him. It felt like he was smothering me; pretending to be a gentleman but actually just taking up all the space around me. And I suppose that's why it feels so good to be away from him. I don't want to be absorbed into Pete like he wants. I want to be me.

I walk up and down the roads that I used to know, looking out over the flat fields and losing myself in them.

I had forgotten how beautiful the light is here; the way it floods across the fields and blazes into the bedroom first thing in the morning. I had forgotten the peace, the silence, the clarity that comes from being out here.

That empty sky melts away my worries and the house works its way back into me. Could it be a friend again?

9

———

ALICE

pril 2005

MA COMES HOME AFTER A WEEK, and I need to get back to the cafe. Marjorie says she'll stop in every day, but Ma is sad and sore. I feel awful leaving her, but I can't leave Soph in the lurch anymore; she has worked eight days straight.

I call Ma every day, and just being with her on the other end of the line feels like inhaling. When I talk to her, I imagine her looking out through the sitting room window at the furrows fading away to the horizon. I can picture the birds taking flight all at once from the wire.

Something is stirring in me; a desire to get back to her, to get back home.

A few days later, I am working in the cafe when Sophie runs in, breathless. She says the hospital just called the flat. Ma has been taken in again. It looks like she has had a stroke.

By the time I ditch Sophie and the cafe again, and get to the hospital, she has slipped into unconsciousness.

The doctors give her a 50/50 chance of survival.

They tell me the postman saw her through the window. She was sitting in an armchair, her back to the window, her arms down by her sides. It wasn't like her to be napping first thing in the morning, he said to the paramedic, and that's how he knew something was wrong. He knocked on the window and she didn't move.

I sit by her side. Her eyelids have a bluish tinge, like fine porcelain.

I take hold of her hand; it is cool to the touch.

She breathes, intermittently.

'Oh Jessie,' I say. 'There was so much I had to tell you.'

I sit there all day with her, but she doesn't wake up again.

At nine pm her rate heart slows. She is leaving, I can feel it.

I fetch the nurses, but they don't leap into action. They nod and say it must be her time. 'If her body's shutting down, there's nothing we can do.'

The helplessness nearly drives me into a blind panic. I can't keep her here with me; all I can do is say sorry and say goodbye.

And in the small hours that night, she dies, right alongside me, accompanied by a symphony of beeps.

There was so much that I hadn't worked out how to say to her. It happened so fast. She was alone, again. And so was I.

Oh, Ma.

Afterwards, I sit there too tired to move, too stunned to cry. I hadn't been able to tell her about how I was thinking of changing everything, how something was calling me back home again.

10

ALICE

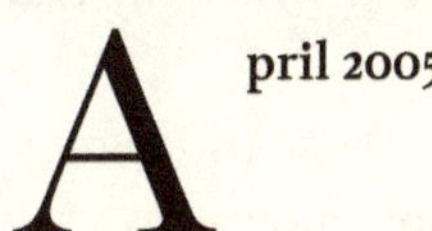 pril 2005

Soph offers to come up to help, even though we both know she can't leave the cafe, but I tell her I'd rather be alone. It's one of those things I need to get through on my own. Marjorie, Ma's friend is here, and she helps me with the arrangements.

Ma's funeral feels so strange: the bright sun and the sight of all the black clothes. There is the nutty smell of suntan lotion in the air, it gleams on people's faces where it hasn't been rubbed in enough.

I feel sick the whole way through the service and don't eat a thing at the wake. It is only in pretending that nothing is out of the ordinary and concentrating on the catering that I can manage. I refill plates of sausage rolls and clear away the empty glasses.

I don't want to reminisce over my mother, not yet. I feel like jealously guarding her; she is mine and no one else's. I talk as little as I can about her, making my excuses if anyone stops me to chat. I didn't know anything of her life. I didn't even know who to invite but, luckily, Marjorie spread the word around the village for me.

Several men cluster under the branches of the apple tree by the shed, clamouring for shade in their formal suits.

And then Vera is there. I am facing the other way, talking to Marjorie as she helps me gather some glasses. There is a hush in the conversation, a slight lull, and I look up, aware that something has happened. I remember her from childhood; she was the farmer's wife on the farm where my dad was poisoned.

She walks up the path in her mud-splattered overalls, through the quietly shocked crowd of mourners. Ma allowed her access through the garden to get to the gate to the field with her horses in it. But today? Right now?

She doesn't look to the right or the left as she walks through. She could be walking down an empty road for all the notice she takes of us. Her hair is done up in one of those old headscarves. She wears a big green coat, despite the heat, her back slightly stooped over and her deep-set dark brown eyes staring straight down at the path in front of her as she walks. Her cheeks are bright red; not with shame, but with years of being out in the baking sun.

'How dare you?' I say, under my breath. But the alcohol gets the better of me and then it's louder. 'How dare you?'

She breaks her stride and slowly turns to me.

'Your farm ruined my ma's life, and you still come here, treading muck through her funeral. How dare you?'

The sound of my voice shocks me but I speak without

thinking. The slur in my speech gives away how much I've had to drink, and so I put my hand to my mouth, to stop myself from saying any more.

She looks at me in the uneasy silence that follows, her flyaway hair waving in the wind. She shakes her head but doesn't say a word, she just looks down and then turns and walks back the way she came. I let her go.

I'm not from here, haven't been here in years. Don't know what the relations are like between the farm and the village now. They didn't used to be good, that's for sure. Just after the accident, when I was little. Ma had to take it out on someone, and, after George had a heart attack out on the fields, she chose Vera.

After a moment of stunned silence, the others turn back to their own conversations. I stand there under the tree, trying to busily arrange glasses on a tray and think myself out of tipsiness. I can feel my heart racing. I don't normally do confrontation – it's not in my nature – but something has come over me.

I can sense someone approaching and look up to see a face that I recognise but haven't seen in years. He has kind eyes and a thick-set face. His hair is wavy and he tucks it behind his ears to keep it in place. He is wearing suit trousers, with a half-untucked shirt. We went to school together, I'm sure.

'It weren't George, though. You know that, don't you?' he says to me.

His hands are leathery and light as he leads me to an empty deckchair in the shade of the house.

'What?' I say, impatiently, looking up at him.

He squats next to me and shades his face from the sun.

'Your dad. It weren't George Burns.'

'It wasn't anyone, I know. It was an accident. But how dare she? Today of all days?'

'It was meant for George, but your dad drank it instead. He told me.'

I stare at him.

'What? Who told you?'

I light a cigarette and listen as the ash creeps along the length of it. I offer one to him and he accepts. I tuck my hair behind my ear and watch him as he talks.

'My friend Leo, he told me, in the greenhouse. I used to go and visit him there. He swore me to secrecy but he's dead now, so I suppose he won't mind.'

'Leo?'

I take a long drag on my cigarette. My mind races.

'Leo killed my father?'

'Oh, I shouldn't have said that, should I? Oh, Alice, I'm sorry, I always say the wrong thing. Not today, I shouldn't have told you. I didn't know if you knew and then I thought I should tell you if you didn't know, but I never know if I'm doing the right thing,' he says, picking at his fingernails.

'Leo? But Leo lived with us. He was like a second father to me. Who are you?' I suddenly say, turning to Christopher. 'How do you know my name? Wait, we went to school together, didn't we?'

He nods.

'I'm Christopher, Marjorie's son.'

'Of course,' I say, vaguely remembering him and his brother playing in the roads and dykes around the village.

'There was a bottle, clear liquid. Your father swigged it. Thought it was water, but it was rat poison. Leo left it there for George.'

'I knew Dad was poisoned, but I've always thought it was an accident. Why would Leo want to poison George?'

'George burned down his brother's house. He told me. The ruins of the cottage on the farm? That's why Leo came here in the first place, to get revenge on him. But it went wrong, and then he couldn't leave. Felt too bad about your mum.'

My mind reels. I'd seen the ruins up by the farm. I'd never thought much of it.

I leave Chris squatting by the deckchair and wander down to the road to stare across the road into the empty field. I'm blown to bits with everything he said; it's too much to take in. Today of all days. Can it be true, that he only ever came to get revenge – Leo, my gentle friend?

I try to swallow all the information down and get back to filling drinks, collecting glasses, and generally busying myself so no one stops to talk to me. I feel sick and my head spins.

As the day cools down, people start to drift away. One by one they come to squeeze my hand between theirs and smile at me.

After everyone has left, Marjorie busies herself walking around the garden with a bin bag, collecting plates and empty plastic cups. There is no time to be sad now, there is too much to do. I start the pile of washing up, leaving the back door open to let the fresh air in.

'Do you remember me from back then?' Christopher says, appearing in the doorway and leaning up against the frame.

'Not really,' I admit. 'How old are you?'

He looks over at his Mum, who says, '27.'

I hesitate before replying.

'I'm ten years older than you. Left when I was seventeen, desperate to see the world. You would have only been seven.'

Marjorie looks at me sharply and then carries on tidying.

It is as if I've said something awful. It's as if the room has swallowed a secret.

Christopher looks like a tourist in a country that is far too hot for him; his shirt untucked, his sleeves rolled up, his top two buttons undone. His tie has separated itself from his shirt and hangs around his neck, its knot hanging against his bare skin.

'Do you remember me?' I ask, turning to scrape the last few sausage rolls into the bin.

He shakes his head and helps himself to another bottle of beer from the counter. He looks around for a bottle opener which I hand to him from the sink. He opens it and takes a swig.

'What did you find then? Was it worth it?'

I look at him, puzzled.

'Oh, when I left? Yeah, I loved it. But I ended up in Cambridge.'

'What's so good about Cambridge?' he says, in defence of the village.

I can't think of anything, so I shrug. 'I just like it.'

Even after helping me to finish all the washing up, Marjorie keeps saying how they must stay, that it isn't right to leave me on my own with all the clearing up to do.

'Please,' I say, 'I'll be fine. I think I'd like to be on my own.'

'Okay then, we'll see you tomorrow?'

I nod.

'Come on, Christopher,' she says, as she walks off down the path.

He dips his head and follows her like a faithful dog, turning to wave as he reaches the road.

There's something that seems a little off about him. He is like an overgrown child, still carrying some sort of innocence that the rest of us have discarded. Strange how he obeys his Mum, unquestioningly.

I walk down to the back of the garden to where the wire fence runs across and the field begins.

Vera's horses are up in the far corner of the field. I light a cigarette and watch them move slowly from one tuft of grass to another. I close my eyes as I breathe in the smoke and then let it out again. The day has finally cooled down.

Everything replays through my mind. I think about Vera and the way I shouted into her blank face. What was I thinking? I think about Leo, his mistake, his regret. I think about Dad, who I never had the chance to know because of that bottle.

I wonder if Ma knew about Leo, knew that the man she welcomed in was the one who took away her husband.

The two horses slowly make their way over to me and I offer them some grass from my side of the fence on an open palm. They take it greedily even though they have a whole field of it for themselves.

'The grass is always greener, hey?' I say to them.

I shiver at the feel of their rough tongues on my palm. I tip back my head to blow my cigarette smoke away from their faces.

When I turn to walk back towards the house it is nearly dark. I can just make out a figure, waiting down by the road. Christopher. His hands are shoved into the front of his jeans pockets and his back is slightly hunched as he stands there.

'You again,' I say, stopping.

We look at each other from either end of the garden.

'Come on,' I say, beckoning him.

I notice that I treat him like a child, just as Marjorie

does. He walks towards me, and we sit on the bench together.

We sit quietly for a while.

'You're home now,' he says.

It annoys me, the way he cuts everything down to the simplest of explanations, as if everything could possibly be that black and white.

'There's no such thing as home,' I say. 'I loved being away from here. I went to London, I went to Corfu, Lisbon, Rome. I had no money and I didn't care. I saw everything. I like my life in Cambridge; I like Sophie, I like the café, I like painting. I have some work up in the cafe and one day I'll have my own show. The village isn't everything, Chris.'

'It's all I need,' he says.

'But how do you know? Have you ever left?' I ask, already guessing the answer.

He shrugs and then takes a cigarette and lights it from mine. The orange tips glow in the dusk and the curls of smoke rise into the sky.

'Been up to Hunstanton a few times. Into Wisbech. Went to Shropshire once, climbed a hill.'

'Christopher,' I say again, placing my hand on his and turning to look at him, 'There's a whole world out there', but already he is smiling and shaking his head.

'For you, maybe,' he says quietly. 'What are you going to do now?'

I shrug, and the tears come to my eyes. My throat constricts and I try to say, 'I don't know,' but it comes out as a whine.

He looks at me awkwardly and puts a hand around my shoulder.

'I'll always look after you, Alice.'

I laugh, despite myself. Here I am being consoled by a stranger. I wipe my hand across my face and stand up.

'I should get some rest. Night, Chris,' I say, leaving him sitting in the dark.

11

ALICE

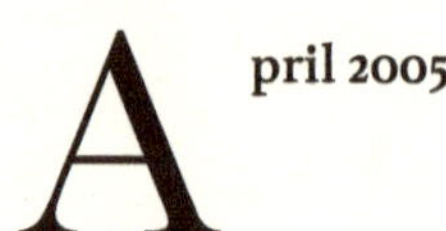

A pril 2005

A FEW DAYS LATER, I wake up knowing I have to get away. I can feel the grasp of the village try to hold me even as I sleep. I suddenly feel choked by the space here, by the silence and the secrets.

As I'm driving out of the village, I see Christopher walking along the road. The city girl in me wants to drive on, pretending I haven't seen him, but country life isn't that convenient. I slow the car to a stop at the roadside. I know he is walking to see me.

'Going already,' he says as a statement, not a question.

'I've got some things to sort out in Cambridge,' I say. 'I'll be back soon.'

He nods.

I drive off and leave him there standing at the side of the road, the guilt thinning out the further I get from him.

Walking into my flat reminds me again of that phone call and Ma's frail voice. I flick through the mail. Nothing for me. I take a shower and lie on the bed, thinking about what Christopher said – that bottle of poison. I wonder what Pete has been doing this last week. He hasn't called me.

Later, I walk down the road to the cafe, where Sophie shouts, 'She's back!' as soon as she sees me.

'When are you coming back to work?' she asks. 'I'm losing the plot here!'

'I could work right now?' I say, vaguely.

'That is the correct answer,' she says and unties her apron before hugging me and handing it over. 'So, how was it?'

'I drank too much and said something stupid. I met someone.'

'What, all at your mother's funeral?

'I realise how ridiculous that sounds.'

'Fill me in later. Look, I need to nip out and pick up some bits. We'll have the boys over for supper now you're back, shall we? Meatballs?'

'Babe, you know Pete and I have split up?'

'Yeah, sure,' she says, faltering, 'but we can still hang out, can't we?'

Before I can answer, she is already out of the door.

That's the problem with being here. Soph has her plans for me. *Fuck*, I think, *now I have to face a dinner with him.*

I busy myself in the café and try thinking through what's next: there's work, there's the ongoing search for a studio, there's a gallery who said they might take some of my paintings. There are things to keep me going.

Later, Pete arrives at the flat with Nick, Sophie's boyfriend. I feel like a ship steering through icy waters. There is nothing I want to say to him, but also I want to be strong enough to exist without him. I breathe deeply and smile at him. We quickly drink enough wine to cover the awkwardness.

'How was it? How are you?' he says and reaches his arms out for a hug.

I can see no way to avoid it and let him hug me, though I want nothing less.

Soph turns up the music and talks loudly.

'Can you imagine living back there, Alice? Back out in the middle of nowhere?' Nick asks me, later.

'No, no, this is home now,' I say, but inside, I'm already thinking of those skies.

'I bet there aren't any other young folks there. What do people do all day?' says Sophie.

'I dunno, look at the sky, get on with things.'

They laugh.

'I think I've always been too scared to go back; it feels so vulnerable, so open to the elements. We're sheltered here, insulated, I guess. I feel smaller there. But that's not a bad thing. I'll be back and forth for a bit; I've got to sort the house out.'

I look down at my wine glass and wonder why the sadness has decided to come now.

'I'm sorry. Do you mind if we talk about something else? It's a lot. Nick, what are you working on?'

I take a large mouthful of red, and it burns as I swallow.

'I'm trying to get a show. I've been thinking about a new piece, photographic, blown up like an Ansell Adams.'

'Sounds good. Any news on studios?'

'The ones at the mill are too much,' Sophie says. 'I just don't make enough and with everything on the line at the café, I haven't got the extra.'

'Oh, we're such dreamers,' I groan. 'How the hell do artists make it work?'

'We do what we were born to do. Things will fall into line, you'll see. You, my friend, are an artist. There's nothing selfish in that,' Pete says, raising a glass.

I clink his glass but don't meet his eyes. I don't believe him.

'But what about real life? Helping people? Doing shit that matters. Can we really justify our existence as artists?'

'Why not?' Pete says, topping up my glass.

It's after twelve when they finally leave.

'Let's do the washing up, I need to talk to you,' I say to Soph, after closing the door on Nick and Pete.

She groans.

We're edging slowly back to sobriety, and I realise I still haven't told her about Leo. We stand in the kitchen and our voices reverberate around the room because it's so small. In front of us, two black panes of glass reflect the yellow light bulb. It's a good flat. I love it because it overlooks a private garden, and for the cocoon that it is - it feels so safe.

'Well, what is it?' she asks, leaning against the counter with her head in her hands.

I realise I can't tell her, there's too much to tell. There's a weight in me; all that I carry, all that I know. I don't know how to make sense of it but now isn't the right time after all. I can't put it into words.

'I missed you, that's all.'

'I missed you too, Al.'

She pulls up the heavy sash window, takes two cigarettes out of a pack and hands one to me. We lean on the worktop and blow our smoke out of the window and into the night like schoolgirls.

. . .

THE NEXT FEW weeks are a time of denial, of ignoring this thing that's pushing up in me. I busy myself in life; I work at the café, making soups and new smoothies, banana loaves and scones.

I try to motivate myself to finish some of my work, but I keep starting new canvases, sketching them out and then losing heart. Closure is hard to come by.

And all the while, an escape route is forming in my mind. I can't stop thinking about the open skies of the fens. It feels like the next step, and it has opened effortlessly in front of me. I think about Pete and wonder if he misses me, if he even cares at all, and it makes me more determined to go.

During my early mornings in the café, I think of what it would be like to be back there. I think of seeing Christopher every day, and I imagine stripping my old bedroom out, back to bare wood, and turning it into a studio. I realise that I would have a rent-free house, and that would mean I could paint full-time. What more would I need except food? I've got about five grand in my savings – enough to see me through a few months – and then there'll be the inheritance, if there's any to come.

And then I swing back the other way. I think I can't do it; I'm not thinking straight. I'm an artist, I need my friends for support, and so I go through the cycle of looking at work-spaces and other jobs, despairing all over again.

But it's there, right in front of me, and the more I try to think about other things, the more obvious it becomes that it is the right thing to do. I mean, I should try it out at least.

There is a growing freedom, too, now that Ma is gone. I loved her like a stone in my chest, but it was a heavy weight, too. It was love mixed with fear, mixed with the feeling that I was disappointing her. That I was never enough for her.

I break it to the guys when I'm ready. It's Sunday morning and Soph and Nick are lying in a bleary-eyed tangle on the sofa. I've already been out to get milk and come back to make tea. I make it loudly in an effort to wake them.

'Guys. It's ten o'clock. I've made you tea,' I say, putting their mugs down on the coffee table.

Nick moans from beneath the duvet he is wrapped up in.

'So, I've decided to move back to Mum's,' I say and wait for the response.

They are quiet. I think maybe they don't think I'll do it.

'It just feels like I have to give it a go, you know?' I say before either of them has spoken.

'That's a bit drastic,' Sophie says, sitting up. 'Are you sure?' She takes a sip of tea and waits a while. 'I mean, it makes sense. I'm just a bit surprised, that's all. What am I going do about the rent?'

'Well, there's someone hiding right there who would kill to live with you. Maybe it'll work for all of us. I'll be bored stiff, but I'll be able to finish a collection for the first time. And I've got three bedrooms, so you can come and stay, right?'

Nick sits up. He looks straight ahead and sips his tea.

'Promise you'll come?'

He grunts again.

'I'll take that as a "yes," Nicholas.'

'What about the cafe?'

'I know, I'm sorry. But you'll find someone. I just have to do this.'

'What will you do for work?'

I shrug.

'Maybe it's a temporary thing, but I've got enough to get me through six months, I think.'

Sophie stands up and reaches her arms around me.

'Okay. I get it. I think you're brave,' she whispers in my ear.

12

ALICE

M ay 2005

I'VE ALWAYS RENTED SO DON'T have much furniture. The few bits I have I leave with Sophie. What I carry with me are useless things, but they're things that make me feel like me: music, books, DVDs, clothes, all my art stuff. My whole life just about fits into my little Ford.

Pete, Nick and Soph are there to say goodbye.

'Soph, these paintings won't fit,' I say, trying to slide them in on top of everything else. 'Can you hang on to them?'

'Sure.'

Maybe it's time to leave my old work behind, I think, as I stack them against the wall and turn from them.

'Pete,' I say, 'I know we didn't really finish things well.'

He shrugs and hugs me.

'Good luck with it all, yeah?' he says, and we end as vaguely as we began.

There is more that I want to say, but I'm not sure what. It could be, 'Come and stay,' or, 'Take care of yourself,' or, 'This doesn't have to be over,' but the words evaporate as I realise that I don't mean any of those things. It's time to start over.

I hug them goodbye, this makeshift and permanently hung-over family of mine, and I climb into the Ford. I blow kisses out of the window as I drive off up the road.

As I'm driving back, and the roads empty out, I realise this is adulthood. I am making a choice, for myself, for the first time. I'm not falling into anything. I am deciding something. It feels good. It feels new.

I pull into the driveway at lunch time. The windows are rolled down, and, when I cut the engine, there is that sweet smell of young grass and manure. I breathe it in. Summer, and a time for new beginnings. I've done it, I think, and inside there is a giddy surge of joy.

As I struggle to get a large bin bag out of the car, I hear a familiar voice shouting out to me.

'You're back!'

I don't have to look up to know it's Christopher. He smiles broadly and seems even happier than I am to be here. His blue checked shirt makes his eyes seem bluer than before and his hair is wild. I suppose he is handsome in a rugged sort of way. I wonder how many times he has walked past my house waiting for me to be here. He takes the black bin bag of clothes from my hand and walks before me up the path to the house.

'You coming home?' he asks.

I nod.

'For a while, at least.'

. . .

It doesn't take me long to unpack. Christopher helps. After we finish, I make tea and stand there leaning against the aga, the one that my mother cooked at, and cleaned down on her knees with a spotted cloth tying back her hair.

'It's good to be back again.'

Christopher nods in agreement and smiles at me. We drink our tea on the lawn outside the house, sitting cross-legged on the grass like kids.

'Why did you leave?' Christopher asks me.

'I just wanted to be away. Is that so bad? I just needed to breathe a bit.'

'But you were all she had.'

I stare at him, wondering if he realises how insensitive that is, but he doesn't seem to notice. True though. Insensitive but true.

He seems distracted and wanders away afterwards, saying he'll come back later.

I wander from room to room, noticing things that I'd forgotten: the ornate lampshade in the bathroom and the ruddy orange tiles on the pantry floor. There is a pile of paper plates on the counter left over from the funeral.

A new feeling washes over me when I wonder if I could make this place my own. If I could clean it down to its bones, and wash away the sadness that has made this house pale. I could paint the lounge bright yellow, and there could be fresh flowers in the kitchen. I want this to be a happy place again like it was in the beginning. Before Dad died. Before I can remember.

The years come tumbling down and I'm that five-year-old, that six-year-old, that seven-year-old, coming home to safety. This is it, the only home I've ever had.

I can't help but think of Ma, alone for all those years. I swallow it down like a stone.

And then I open the windows and dream.

Maybe I can paint myself here, remake myself here? Maybe I can find who I've been waiting to be all this time? I look out of the open window to the field beyond and feel giddy with joy at the chance of a new start.

It feels for once that anything is possible.

13

ALICE

May 2005

THE FIRST THING I do is to take in the space. I notice the colours and the way the light falls in each room. I see the light in my old bedroom is perfect for a studio, but I resist ripping things out for now.

I walk a lot. I watch the starlings all in a row on the telegraph wires. I smell the earth and feel grounded here. I walk out to the Wash, along past the lighthouses, high up on the bank, where the wind buffets me in the face and takes my breath away.

Sophie comes up for the weekend a few weeks later and, by the time she arrives, I'm itching to get started.

I fetch her from King's Lynn on Friday night. When she steps from the train, her hair dishevelled, I smile.

'I fell asleep!' she yells into the darkness.

'Come here, you daft twat,' I say, and hug her tightly.

'This is a god-forsaken place, isn't it?' she says.

'It's not that bad! I miss you, babe.'

'We miss you, too.'

Back at the house I cook her a chicken curry out of a jar and ask about life in Cambridge.

'Nick is good. The cafe is good. Haven't seen Pete. But sod that. This! You gave up Cambridge for this?'

'Ha! Yes.'

'Shall we get to work?' she says, pushing her plate away from her once she's finished. 'Make me a coffee, I've got energy. I've got cover for the cafe until Monday morning so use me while you've got me.'

'Let's do it. There's plenty of clearing to do, but the studio's the main thing. Let me show you around.'

She follows me into the dining room, where mine and Mum's two chairs are still pulled up to the fire. The dining table is pushed against the sideboard. We go through to the formal sitting room which is draughty and which Ma never used.

Upstairs, I show her the three bedrooms, mine as a child, Leo's, which was a box room, and Ma's room on the end.

'The view from here,' I say, 'I love it, just sky and fields. And the light.'

I knew it would do me good to have Sophie here. She believes in my strangest plans; she is faithful and unquestioning.

We begin by dragging things from under my bed. There's a blue suitcase stuffed full of letters from me and a few from Dad to Ma.

'What's this, Al?' she says as she flicks through a notebook, full of tight handwritten scrawl.

I try to read some and immediately, I know who wrote it.

'My God, it's Leo's,' I say. 'Soph, listen:

I WAS BORN A WANDERER; the road always calling me. These skies, vast and full, are with me wherever I am. Full of storm or the brightest blue, of wind that blasts across the black mud, they are my constant companion ... What are things but weight on a man's shoulders? The skylarks have it right; singing their way through the day, not a stitch on their backs.

'THE THING I wanted to tell you, Soph, the other day, when we were washing up drunk, was that Chris told me that Leo killed my father. It was an accident, a bottle of poison meant for George, the landowner, but my dad swigged it instead, and it killed him. It was all just a stupid accident. I bet it's in here.'

'Leo's the guy who lived with you and your mum when you were little, right?'

I nod.

'Who's Chris?'

'He's the guy I met. You'll meet him soon enough.'

'A guy?' she says, one eyebrow raised.

I shake my head.

'Not that kind of a guy, more like a kid brother kind of guy.'

I sit there on the floor of the bedroom and read the diary while Sophie unpacks the wardrobe, spreading its contents on the floor. I read some bits aloud to her:

.   .   .

ONE NIGHT, I'm sitting in my deckchair, about to fall into my evening snooze, when I hear her.

'Felt like a walk, didn't we Alice?' she says.

'Well, do you want to stop for a bit?' I ask her.

'I can't imagine living like this,' she keeps saying. 'There's really nothing else you want?'

By the time she's thinking about leaving, it is dark. Alice has fallen asleep on her knee, wrapped in my old blanket. I walk her back home, steering her across the black fields.

I CLUTCH it to my chest, this tattered diary.

'It's me,' I gulp. 'This book holds me inside its pages.'

Sophie starts to peel wallpaper from the walls. It's barely attached anymore, so comes away in great swathes. I read snatches aloud to her as she works:

THERE IS something about walking over an open field in the dark that I don't like, even with the lantern. It's the way that the light makes you blind in the darkness.

IT IS A SWEET DAY, quiet with almost no sound. So different this place can be, summer to winter, spring to autumn, and I marvel at it. Today is a kind day, the kind where the earth rises up and blesses you just because it can; because it is in its nature.

'LEO!' she says, drying her hands on a cloth as she opens the door. She smiles at me. She's wearing one of those aprons that tie around the middle; it is covered in red and white checks. Her hair is tied back from her face.

I BRING her some apples after church. She breathes in as they pass under her nose, and I watch the way she moves; the way her skirt swims around her as she turns. It makes me feel dizzy.

'HE LOVED HER,' I say. 'I never knew. Of course he loved her, it's so obvious.' I put the book down and lean back against the wall feeling history being rewritten under me. Then I open it again and keep reading:

MAY, the miracle month; the scent of the first blossom, the hope of summer, shoots of wild green unfurling. A welcome sight after all that winter. Alice turns seven today. I remember when she was just a dot. Her mother insisted I come to the party. I made her a little bird, carved from a piece of wood back at my greenhouse.

'OH, this bit is from when he moved in. I remember it. He was so awkward.'

I CAN'T GET USED to the comfort and the quiet up here where she's put me. It's a different kind than I'm used to. It's not in any way the same as the rush of wind through the grass, the hum of a car going by at the back of a field, two miles over, the murmur of footsteps passing or the hush of far-off voices. The quiet I know is one that's full of life. In my greenhouse, I was close to the outside; the fresh air wove its way in through the cracked panes of glass as I slept and formed a second skin. Green roots pushed up through the sacking that made my rough bed and I smelt the earth all night long.

In a field, there are many ways to cross and each time the carpet is different. There might be a coin, glinting in the soil, or the rustle of a small creature moving away. In the field, the wallpaper is the sky. It comes right down to the ground, full of colour and mood all day long.

There's the clear sun up with the tufts of puffy cloud floating by, and the red wings of the sun settling back down over the land at the end of the day, spreading their glow over the furrows. Then there are other days, the ones when the clouds are drawn across the sky like fine white scars. It seems that everything would come from that sky: the news of the weather, the end of the world, the sadnesses that fall like rain.

And that's what amazes me, and what gives me hope. After the day you think might be the worst in your life, the next morning, the sky is there to wake you up, to make you see again.

And each day the sky starts again, as empty, as graceful as it ever had been.

Almost as if it didn't know, almost as if you could forget.

Even the day after you killed a man.

'OH MY GOD,' Alice says. 'He confesses to it right here.'

·   ·   ·

'TELL ME ALL ABOUT JIM,' she says one day. 'I'll pay you good money to write down everything he ever said, all his jokes.'

And so, I'm putting it all down here.

There's just one tale that I need to tell, to set it out plain so as folks know the truth. Well, Jessie, it's for you, really. I can't tell you to your sweet face, so I'll tell it to this paper in the hope that you'll find it one day. It was me that killed Jim. I didn't mean to. Edward Sedgwick was my brother; he was burned out of the village by the Burns. And I came wandering, to get revenge. And I thought to come here, to teach George a lesson. To take down the tallest tower. So, I went early to the shed. I found the bottle of strychnine and decanted it into a plain bottle. George were there with us at morning break and I'd swapped it with his bottle. These things happen all the time on farms. I wanted to give him a taste of his own medicine. But he didn't take another swig and then he didn't come at lunch, and it just stood there in the grass. I forgot all about it. And then Jim picked it up and I was looking the other way. When I turned, and realised, my heart fell to the floor. I couldn't undo it, Jessie, no matter what I did. I'm so sorry.

AND IT ALL unfolds before me, the reason he came to the village, and his guilt forever afterwards.

'Mum must have known. She never told me. She must have thought I'd never forgive him if I knew.'

'I believe him,' says Sophie, after I've finished. 'Do you? That it was an accident, like he says?'

'Yes, I do,' I say. 'Do you think I ought to hate him?'

'No. He loved you both. You know that much. And like he says, it was an accident.'

'I haven't got the energy to be angry with him. It would unpick my childhood. I want things left as they were.'

'I get that,' she says.

By midnight we have got all the furniture out of the room and bagged up my childhood dresses. We do it quickly, leaving no time for remorse.

We drag the wardrobe downstairs and into the garden, and then my pink bed frame. We are exhausted but don't stop. This is what I need Sophie here for. I would have been bogged down in memory otherwise. We keep going until 3 am.

The next morning, when we emerge for breakfast, there are bags and bags on the lawn. I'll sort it later, before it rains, I think. I'm impressed by how much we got done last night, and we drink our morning coffee in a daze before we start off again.

We finish peeling away the wallpaper and roll back the carpet. Underneath, we find beautiful floorboards. I take down the awful curtains and leave the window bare.

We sit down to a simple lunch of ham sandwiches and fruit cake, washed down with several mugs of strong tea.

'Let's have a walk before we get started again, shall we? I need a ciggie. I need you here longer than this weekend, Sophie! There's so much to do!'

We walk up the main street of the village and turn left along World's End Lane.

'I told you it was the end of the world,' Sophie laughs.

We turn the corner and there is Christopher, sitting on the edge of the curb, his legs sticking out into the road.

'Christopher!' I say and instinctively rush towards him. 'Are you okay?'

He looks up and smiles. 'I'm looking for Whitey. Who's this?' he says, pointing at Sophie.

'This is my good friend, Sophie.'

'Will you be my friend, too?' he asks and holds out a hand towards her.

She looks at his dirty fingernails and hesitates.

'Sure,' Soph says, keeping her hands in her pockets.

Christopher frowns, gets up and walks along with us a little way.

'What are you doing today, Christopher?'

'Just walking, seeing what's what.'

We walk to the outskirts of the village and end up walking back past his mother's house.

'Why don't you go home?' I say. 'Let your mum know you're okay.'

'Okay,' he says. 'Would that be a good idea? Ain't my home though, I got the caravan.'

'Oh, where's that?'

'Down the garden. Want to see?'

Sophie shoots me a warning look.

'Not just now, we've got too much work to do. Soon, though?'

He nods and then turns, his shoulders slumping as he trudges down the lane towards his mum's house.

Sophie and I walk on.

'What's up with him?' she asks.

'I'm not sure,' I reply. 'He's like a child, but he knows what's what, told me the truth about Leo, didn't he? Socially awkward. Has hardly left the village.'

'Poor sod,' Sophie laughs.

We spread dust sheets over the floor and begin to paint the walls white. A white space is what I most want; a space that's mine and mine alone, and here it is, coming into being before my eyes. We have covered all the walls and the ceiling by dinner time.

After we eat, we do another coat. We leave it to dry for an hour then I take up the dust sheets, though the walls are still sticky to the touch. I pull in the armchair from Ma's bedroom. I set my easel up opposite the window and bring in my cardboard box full of oils. I open the window wide and turn the lights off.

On Monday, I will walk in here and it will be ready. I will have all I need: my paints, an open window, the sky. A shimmer of excitement rises. A mouthful of guilt, too, that I swallow down.

SUNDAY, we sleep late. After breakfast, I take Soph to the station. We're both exhausted.

'Take care, won't you? Thank you for everything. I love you!'

The train pulls out of the station, and I cry a little as she goes.

MONDAY, I'm up early, waking with butterflies dancing in my stomach. I put on my bright blue shirt, my paint-splattered dungarees and my old boots. I go down to the kitchen, feeling thankful for this change that has come up in my life.

I paint in a fury. My square of canvas is the sky, each day a new thing, just like Leo said.

I reach for his diary again, and I read the words, tattooed on the page in his uneven scrawl:

EACH DAY the sky starts again, as empty, as graceful as it ever had been. Almost as if it didn't know, almost as if you could forget.

. . .

AND I PAINT ANYWAY. For his grief, for me, for Ma, for all that cannot be changed. But also for the sky, new every day.

I put a pot of coffee on the stove and turn to look out over the yard to the field. The early sunlight picks out the cobwebs and turns them silver. As the coffee bubbles up in the pot and fills the room with its rich and wonderful smell, I cut a slice of bread and spread it with butter and strawberry jam. You could never get bread this soft in Cambridge. I shovel it into my mouth quickly, leaning on the counter and looking out of the window. No need to sit to eat; no time to waste. There is no horizon in my day now except for the new canvas, waiting to come into being.

I take my mug of coffee upstairs and throw open the window to see the field of wheat and silver in the early morning light. It moves like a sea, grey and undulating. I take my paintbrush and begin to sketch.

14

ALICE

M ay 2005

THE NEXT MORNING, I am lead. I can't get up. I can't stop
crying. Ma is never coming back, and I am wiping her out of
this house with glee. What a selfish human being I am. She
gave me everything, her whole self, and what have I done in
return?

My legs have no strength. I lie there in Ma's bed,
watching the sun rise in the east, spread its wings through
the field, and then begin to dip down towards the horizon at
the end of the day. I manage to get up to go to the loo and
that's it. No ciggies, no food. I feel wretched. My stomach
hurts and my eyes are sore from crying. I doze on and off. I
dream of Ma and I think of Pete. I miss Soph and the cafe.

I spent myself gutting it, now I wish I hadn't been so
ruthless.

She's never coming back.

ALICE

June 2005

A FEW WEEKS LATER, I'm on my hands and knees, a scarf tied around my hair like Ma used to, cleaning out the Aga when Marjorie calls, 'Anybody there?' through the window. She has a habit of turning up unexpectedly, a bit like her son.

She bustles her way in, with armfuls of useless things that she thinks I might want.

'I found these in the cupboard under the sink,' she says, handing me some old plastic pegs. 'I thought you might be able to use them, seeing as you don't have any of your own.'

It's irritating but endearing how much she notices about my life, and how much she takes it upon herself to correct things for me.

'And you said you wanted to start growing your own veg. Have you dug the plot over yet?'

'No, I haven't got around to it,' I say, thinking of the canvas waiting for me upstairs.

'Well, I hope I'm not intruding, it's just that I've brought my spade and can give you a hand, if you'd like. It's a bit late, but if we get going you could have some salad growing in a month or so.'

'Oh gosh, Marjorie, I'm not very organised... Should we dig it over now, then?' I ask, assuming that's what she wants to hear.

She nods and hands me the spade. As I reluctantly follow her outside, I'm still thinking of finishing that painting, and the way the sun melted over the field last night and filled the bedroom with its glow, but I have to remind myself she's only trying to help.

WE BEGIN to dig over the veg plot. Mum hadn't sown anything this year but there was some spinach left over from last year that was still going strong. But I can't get away from the view. It strikes me that I might paint a picture for each day of the year or one at each hour of the day. I like the thought of something so meticulous, so planned; as if you could ever pin the sky down.

As if by instinct, Christopher turns up and joins in. With his help, we make light work of it and by the end of the morning, we have sowed rows of lettuce, rocket and carrots, and even put in some seed potatoes.

By the time we have finished, Chris has disappeared again.

I've noticed he suddenly switches off sometimes and wanders away like he's just remembered he's got something important to do.

It's thirsty work and I go to the kitchen to fetch us a

drink. Marjorie follows me and hovers nervously at my elbow, while I make tea.

'Are you okay, Marjorie?'

'Well, love, to tell you the truth, I'm not okay. It's Christopher.'

She has been waiting for me to ask her.

'What's he done?'

'It's more a case of what he's not done, love. He doesn't bring me his washing anymore, and I just can't do it, going down there, invading his privacy, going through his things. God knows what he's got in that caravan; there's a stench coming off it. He's not been looking after himself for a long time. It all goes back to Cassie. You know about that, don't you, love? I just don't know what to do for him.'

I take a sip from my tea and look at her over the rim of the mug. I can tell there's more that she doesn't know how to come out with. I'll ask Chris about Cassie later, I think.

'I know you've only just moved back, but I thought you might be a positive influence. It's just you're friends, sort of, and what with you being younger than me and all, I thought you might take him under your wing, a bit. I've got money. I'll pay you to help out with him.'

'Gosh, I don't want your money. I can see he needs help, but I don't know if I'm the right one to give it. I'm not trained or anything.'

'But he likes you, and that's half the battle. I'm too old. I dread to think what'll happen when I'm gone.'

'Don't talk like that, Marjorie,' I say.

'It's got to be talked about,' she says. 'What will happen to him? We thought he'd grow out of this.'

'I understand your worry but, I don't know...' I trail off.

'All I'm asking is that you check on him from time to

time,' she says, looking at me. I know she's asking for a lot more than she says.

'He doesn't need to know that you're being paid,' she adds. 'Let him think you're a friend.'

'I am a friend. You're not paying me.'

I take a sip of my tea and wonder what she is really asking me.

Sometimes it feels as if this life is chosen for you.

CHRISTOPHER TURNS up a few days later and we sit on the front lawn together. His hair has taken on the colour of the sun.

I look at him differently in the light of all that Marjorie has said. It doesn't look like he has washed in a long time. His jeans have been stained by layer upon layer of dirt. I wonder how long he's worn them for. His body carries a musty tang of dried sweat and earth. I make him a coffee and offer him a cigarette.

He asks me again why I left the village, and I disappear upstairs to find pictures of the flat in Cambridge and of Sophie and the guys.

He studies them intensely. It seems like he is trying really hard to understand something.

'I love Cambridge, it's a beautiful city – have you ever been?' I babble. 'I used to like walking home at the end of a night shift at the hospital or walking out first thing in the morning when it felt like the city was beginning to stir. I liked the thought that I was surrounded by lots of people, for some reason. Made me feel less alone, I suppose.'

'When you were there,' Christopher asks, 'did you miss Jessie? Did you just forget about her?'

'I suppose I didn't want to be needed.'

He looks at me vacantly.

'And what did your house smell like?' he says.

'I lived with Sophie – you met her the other day. I'd sometimes buy fresh flowers from the market, so maybe it smelled of that. Or the meals that me and Sophie cooked. I didn't cook very well – didn't have the time when I worked at the hospital. Tomatoey, I suppose. We ate lots of pasta. Sophie is great. I work for her now, I did, at her cafe. Or paint, perhaps it smelt of my oil paints. I paint. That's why I've moved back – to find the time to paint.'

'Mum said you worked in a hospital.'

'I was a nurse for eleven years, but it was too hard. I couldn't make everyone better. So, I left. Worked in a cafe. Not so difficult on the soul.'

He stares hard at me for a moment as if I have said something wrong, and then he snaps out of it and looks down.

'You helped people to get better.'

'Yes, but sometimes things don't work out. People don't always get better.'

He nods.

'Who's Cassie?' I ask, tentatively.

He looks at me square in the face.

'She's my best friend.'

'What happened to her?'

'She went missing.'

'Oh God, that's awful, Christopher, I'm so sorry.'

'I miss her so much.'

'Did they find her?'

He shakes his head.

'Shit,' I say.

'When did she go missing?'

'Must be twenty years ago. She was seven.'

We sit there in quiet, for a while, this enormous truth dumped between us. No wonder he's messed up, I think.

'I like painting,' he suddenly says, pulling up blades of grass with his fingers one by one. 'Can you teach me?'

'Sure.'

'Can you teach me right now?' he asks.

'Why not?' I say.

We go up to the studio and I open the window. I start with the basics.

'Look out of the window. Do you see the shape? That line of poplars, that cloud in the sky. It's framed beautifully, isn't it? The way the wheat moves like waves on an ocean. I paint this every day, Christopher. Maybe I'm going insane, but I think it's so beautiful.'

He looks out of the window.

'I'll work here, and you work there,' I say and set him up with a canvas and an easel while I continue to work on one that I've already started.

'A good way to start is to mix raw sienna, that's this colour, with a little turps and paint it on really thin and then sketch out what you want to paint. We'll cover all this up later.'

He nods, takes a brush and starts sketching. He is absorbed, sketching out the shapes of the clouds with precision.

'You've done this before, haven't you?'

'No.'

'Really? Well. Wow.'

He sketches out the sky, the white of the clouds, the reedy sea, the white cracks, the haze. I look at him while he works, and he is lost within it.

'And now we need to take a break,' I say. 'That needs to dry for two days before we can carry on'.

'Two days?'

He looks bereft.

'We can always go and sketch some more right now, though. Have you used charcoal before?'

'No, but I've always liked drawing, Alice. Mum used to say I was good at it.'

'You are good at it, Christopher.'

We walk out to the back of the Burns' farm and sit on an old tractor and look out to the horizon.

He comes alive in the place and sketches quickly, capturing the mellowing sun and the shape of the clouds.

I look at him, this half-man, half-boy, and wonder why we have been thrown together like this.

Two days later, he knocks at the door, desperate to finish his canvas. I lead him up to the studio.

'Now you can fill in the main blocks of colour. This is a good choice for the soil,' I say, mixing the colours for him. 'Remember that the deepest shadows are the closest to you. As you get further from the object, the paler it will appear.'

I leave him on his own in the studio and go up to find him later. He has painted an angry picture, rain falling onto the fields, clouds being pulled this way and that in the sky. It is full of storm, full of emotion. It doesn't match the view out of the window at all.

In the clouds, in the right-hand corner, it looks like there is a face.

'Who's that?' I ask.

'Just the clouds,' he says looking straight at me.

But it is her, I know it is, the one that he lost.

16

ALICE

June 2005

IT ALL CHANGES a few weeks later when he shows up in the dark, his face pressed against my window, telling me his mother has collapsed.

After we run back to his mother's house, we wait in darkness outside the kitchen door while the paramedics fill in their paperwork and then cover Marjorie in a sheet to take her away.

I ask Christopher if he wants to come back to mine for a while instead of staying in the caravan.

Shadows cross his face, and I can see him trying to take hold of the shape of his life now that everything has changed.

He seems just like a child.

He nods.

I walk with him up to the back of the garden, where his caravan is lodged in the hedgerow like some gigantic bird's nest. I stand at the doorway feeling like a mother at the threshold of her teenage son's room, not wanting to go in, unsure as to what she might find.

Every surface is littered with the detritus of life: receipts, teabags, shoes, cups, crisp packets. It smells of damp and the sour tang of black mould. He grabs a carrier bag from the floor and starts shoving into it all the essentials he can think of. I call out useful items from the doorway – 'Shoes, toothbrush, socks' – as he runs around gathering odds and ends as if he is on a scavenger hunt.

By the time we have walked back to mine, it is late and there isn't much left to be said. I ring his brother Ben. We've never spoken before.

'Hi. It's Alice. I live in the village. I'm a friend of Christopher's.'

'Is he okay?'

'Christopher's fine ... It's your mum. She had a stroke this afternoon. Christopher found her in the house. We called an ambulance, but ... it was too late.'

'Let me talk to Christopher,' Ben says, matter-of-factly, and I wonder if he has heard what I just said.

I hold the phone out, but Christopher shakes his head.

'He doesn't want to talk just now,' I say. 'I'm sorry.'

I know what it is like to hear news like this over the phone, to have your thoughts spooling out in your brain: When did it happen? Why wasn't I there to help? How long had she been lying there?

Ben is vague, half-there.

'I'll drive over in the morning,' he says.

'I'm sorry, Ben. Okay. Night.'

. . .

'HE WASN'T ALWAYS LIKE THIS,' Ben says. 'He was happy.'

He is standing in the kitchen, leaning up against the counter, and we are clutching mugs of tea to our chests. Chris was up early and went out wandering. We haven't even talked about Marjorie yet.

Ben is taller than Chris, and a little thinner, but they have the same eyes.

'There was one day when we all rode out to the Wash together: Cassie, Christopher and me. The sky was perfect. We left our bikes in a pile at the gate and ran along the high banks of the Nene, past the pair of white lighthouses. We sat out at the end of the path staring out over the Wash. He was happy and carefree. After Cassie, everything changed.'

'Christopher told me about her. Awful.'

'Yeah. I mean, life just stopped for him.'

Just then the back door bursts open and Christopher runs in holding a rabbit with its head smashed in. His eyes dart from one of us to the other; he doesn't even say, 'Hi,' to Ben.

'Chris!' I say. 'Are you okay?'

'He was on the road, I thought I could warm him up a little; give him some milk.'

'Chris, you can't bring back to life what is already dead.' I look at him. 'Shall we put him outside and bury him later?'

He stares coldly at me, shakes his head and runs around the back of the house with the rabbit clutched to his chest.

'Ben's here,' I call out, but he doesn't come back.

Ben and I finish our cups of tea and stand there awkwardly, wondering what to do next.

'I'm so sorry about Marjorie. It's such a shock. She was here a few days before, helping me to dig over the vegetables.'

'Mmm,' he murmurs. 'I haven't really taken it in.'

He still looks baffled, talking about his mother. Almost as if he had forgotten that that's why he is here.

'Shall we walk over to the house? We might find Christopher.'

We walk together down World's End Lane and along Common Way to his childhood home.

'So, who are you?' Ben asks.

I laugh.

'I'm Jessie's daughter. I've been away for twenty years. Moved back after my mother died in March. Fell into a sort of friendship with Christopher. Your mum asked me to keep an eye on him. I feel like she knew she was going to go.'

'I wish she'd told me. Perhaps he's in the caravan.'

We walk down the garden, past the old outhouse, the crumbling sheds and the bowed hedgerow. Long brambles snake out across the lawn, trying to reclaim what was once theirs.

We can hear things being moved around in the caravan. We approach and wait at the doorway. Christopher is pulling pieces of crumpled paper out of a bag and throwing them over his head.

'Hey Chris,' Ben shouts, and Christopher turns to see him.

'Ben,' he says, turning to look at him and then back to what he was doing.

Ben looks embarrassed.

'Shall I leave you two to it?' I say, but Ben seems already defeated.

'No, stay,' he mouths to me, shaking his head.

Ben approaches Christopher and says, 'Mate, what are you looking for?' and sits down next to him on the beige sofa.

Christopher shrugs.

'I'm not sure. Mum left me instructions somewhere, and I can't remember where. Telling me what to do if ... if ...'

'It's okay. You don't need to say it.'

Christopher looks at Ben and his face crumples. He falls onto him, and Ben wraps his arm around his back and holds him.

'What did you do with the rabbit?'

'Chucked it in the hedge. Its head was all bashed in. He wasn't coming back.'

LATER THAT EVENING, when we are back at mine, Christopher realises that his brother has driven halfway across the country for him, and he turns to talk to him.

I leave them to talk while I prepare dinner and eavesdrop. They are so different to each other.

'So, are you here often, then?' Ben says to Christopher.

'I live here.'

'Do you?' Ben says, surprised.

I shout back through the doorway, 'He doesn't live here, he just stayed last night.'

'I stayed in your bed, didn't I, Alice?'

'Yes, you slept there because you were cold, but then I slept down here on the sofa, didn't I?'

I try to compose myself and put the kettle on the Aga. More tea. I can feel my face flushing. What must Ben think of me?

'He was upset,' I explain. 'We found your Mum and then I called you. He didn't want to go back to the caravan on his own.'

'So, he slept in your bed?'

'Well, it sounds weird when you say it like that. Nothing happened, I'm just trying to be there for him.'

. . .

'LITTLE BROTHER,' Ben sighs, 'I'm so sorry that you found Mum like that.'

I watch from the doorway and notice that Chris can't handle being looked at full in the face. He breaks Ben's gaze, stands up and walks out of the room.

When we eat together – chicken pie and gravy – the air is like ice between them. I wonder what happened. I wonder if Christopher knows how to have relationships. I babble nervously to fill in the awkwardness.

Ben and Christopher both stay in the spare room, making up makeshift beds with sofa cushions.

WHEN BEN IS GETTING ready to go the following night, he turns to Chris.

'Have you thought about a break, about coming to stay? Anna and the children would love to see you.'

'But how will I get back?' he says nervously.

'I don't think he could get on a train,' I interject. 'You'd have to bring him back.'

'Come for a weekend then? I could drive you back on a Sunday night. Why don't you come and live with us for a while, Chris?'

'Have you asked your wife about this?' I laugh.

'No, I haven't asked Anna. But I can't leave you here with a stranger. No offence, Alice, you've done a lot for us, but Chris isn't your family. You don't owe him anything.'

Christopher looks at me.

'Ben, she's my best friend,' Christopher says, and I feel strangely proud, even though it's not remotely true. We hardly know each other.

'I'm not a stranger, Ben. Christopher is happy here. Leave him here with me.'

As the words are coming out of my mouth, I wonder what I am saying. Ben bristles at this. He follows me into the kitchen to try to talk to me.

'He's my brother. I know what's best for him.'

'Do you?' In the few months I have known Christopher, all I have learned of his brother is that he isn't there. 'He needs to be here, in the village. This is all he knows.'

'But I don't even know you.'

'And I don't know you. Look, I know he needs help. But he is still an adult. You have to take his wishes into account. He's not a child anymore.'

'He's not really an adult either,' Ben says in a low voice.

'I'm not taking advantage of him. Nothing happened last night; he was just scared. I want the best for him, as I'm sure you do, too. It has to be his choice though, doesn't it?

The front door slams.

Ben moves to go after Christopher, into the night, but I say, 'Look, you can't stop him. He wanders. That's just what he does.'

'I can't take him if he doesn't want to come but I just think he needs more support than this. No one is asking you to take on Christopher, he's not your responsibility.'

'Well, that's not quite true. Like I said, Marjorie spoke to me about it before she died.'

'Why are you taking this on? Why do you think you can fix him when no one else has been able to?'

'It's better this way. You have your life to get on with, we're fine, me and Christopher. We'll be okay.'

'But you've got your own life to lead.'

'Maybe there's room enough for Christopher too,' I shrug.

Ben is lost for words. He turns from me, walks briskly down the path, and drives away.

I miss Marjorie already and curse her for leaving me with the great responsibility of looking after this man who doesn't know how to live. But now here is Ben, offering to take it from me and I am saying no. Perhaps I like being needed, in however small a way. Surely, I can still make my art and be here for Christopher, too?

TWO WEEKS LATER, I'm nibbling sandwiches in the garden at Marjorie's funeral. Why does it have to be such a nice day? Ben and Anna's children are chaotic and lovely as they play chase in the garden, and I stand there watching, wondering again if I will ever have children of my own.

Ben turns to Anna, pointing at their youngest, Noah, and whispers into her ear. He turns to her in the sun and runs his hand ever so lightly over her hip. It sends a pang through my heart.

Even though there is all this movement round about them, there is a flame still there at the heart of them; not of desire, but of intimacy. Of knowing. I look for Christopher and he is laughing loudly with Sam, their other son, in the willow.

I hang around the edges of the funeral, trying to make myself busy in the background. I'm not one of the family. Ridiculously, I find that I am jealous of Anna for almost everything about her: her perfect life, her beautiful children, Sam, Lucie, and Noah, her hair, her husband who loves her.

Later on, I approach her, trying to appear normal and unintimidated.

'Hi, I'm Alice, Chris' friend.'

She smiles perfectly.

'Nice to meet you.'

'Look, I just wanted to say, I'm not trying to take advantage of Chris. I can help him; I have the time for him. It works okay.'

'I don't judge you,' she says, smiling at me, touching me on the arm. 'We are amazed that you can connect with him.'

She pauses.

'Ben can come across as a bit ... abrupt. That's just him. Don't worry about it. We're so thankful, Alice. I don't think Chris is ready for a relationship though.'

'Good grief. I'm not offering him a relationship; I'm helping him get through.'

'But you've got your own life to lead, no one is asking you to give that up for Chris. We can get him the help he needs.'

And suddenly I feel like a dogsbody, a carer; someone who is mopping up the spillage so they can get on with their wonderful lives. I feel my face flush, and, against my will, I find myself confiding in her. It's this thing I do when I meet intimidating women.

'I don't know why I've taken it on. I didn't choose to; he seemed to take me on.'

'That's just the way it is sometimes,' she says.

'I mean what if I am the help he needs?'

'Well, yeah, maybe you are. But it's your choice at the end of the day. And you need to tell us if it gets too much.'

And I smile, and I see that this is a crossroads. I say yes or no. My whole life depends on it. I make an excuse and head off to do something else, like I always have, or I stay and see this through.

But it isn't as clean-cut as that. I am already interwoven

into this plot. Christopher has told me more about my life than I ever knew, and I've only known him for a couple of months. I already know I won't leave.

17

ALICE

ugust 2005

FOR A WHILE, he lives in between. He comes and goes, and I don't know what to do with him. Is he mine? Is he my responsibility? Should I tell him off? Set him boundaries? Let him roam? He wanders the village looking for his mother, looking for Cassie. He sleeps in the caravan some nights, some nights at mine.

'Why don't you sleep at your Mum's, Christopher?' I ask him when we are out wandering together.

'Mum kicked me out,' he answers, sheepishly.

'But she's not here anymore.'

He shrugs. He won't ever go against her.

The birds won't come into roost, and it is one of those nights that hangs open, no one settling to sleep. Our shoes are loud on the tarmac of the quiet roads that we walk upon.

'What do you want to do when you're older, Christopher?'

He looks disoriented; almost shocked at the word 'older.'

'I have to choose?' he says, looking at me, anxiously.

I nod.

'Imagine you could do anything you wanted. What would you do?'

He shrugs.

'I don't know, Alice. Can't see nothing, really. Just want to make everything right again.'

'There's something good waiting for you Christopher, I know it.'

We keep walking.

18

THE VILLAGE

August 2005

ANOTHER NIGHT and we watch Christopher as his boots click along our tarmac spine. Not a thing in either direction. He has been in the Five Bells for hours. Around and around in circles, he goes. Trying to grow up but she holds him back; not wanting to grow, not wanting to leave her.

But now, he doubles over, hands to his knees and vomits. It pools and glimmers under the streetlamp.

'Urgh,' he groans. 'One too many.'

We know it was many too many.

He pushes himself up to standing again but the dizziness sends him stumbling backwards into the steep-sided dyke. His body slams back against the earth, his feet wet through.

He giggles gently, and then pulls himself up with a handful of reeds and rolls into the field on the other side. He crushes the plants beneath him, and looks up at the cloud-less sky, waiting for stars.

He drifts off to sleep there in the field, but then a fresh gust of wind wakes him, pressing his shirt to his chest and making him shiver.

Then, suddenly, he sits up, as if remembering something.

'Cass,' he says.

He stands up and repeats her name before he turns and sets off across the field at a run, stumbling over the furrows.

We sigh, shake our heads, rattle our bones.

Again, again, again. Around in circles, it goes.

He crawls under the yellow tape and fumbles at the caravan door in the darkness. He pulls the cord for the light, and an electric glare lights up the room. He almost comes back to the day, to the truth. He pauses for a breath of air and then goes under again.

The poster that he has already started is on the table. He sketched out her face earlier, and, looking at it again, he thinks it looks about right; she had that sparkle in her eye. It makes his heart lurch inside his chest to see her face. He sits down.

'WHERE ARE YOU?' he has written at the top of the page in capital letters. He has retraced the letters three times in black biro but now he thinks they look too menacing. He tilts his head this way and that to try to decide whether the layout looks right.

He sighs loudly, tears away the page and screws it up, aiming it at the plastic bag hanging from one of the kitchen drawers. There are paper cannonballs all around the bag, in the sink and on the floor.

'This is taking too long, it'll be too late,' he whispers, rubbing his eyes.

His knee jogs nervously up and down underneath the flimsy table and some of the letters have started to come out shaky, so he reaches under the table to try to steady himself. He picks up a half-eaten pasty left out from yesterday and eats it quickly, dropping flakes of pastry on the table.

Christopher is still in his twenties, but he looks older. His thick bushy hair has a slight curl; it is unruly and sticks out above his ears. His cheeks are ruddy and his skin is cracked and dry from the outside air. He has a broad farmer's back and wears a checked shirt.

He starts to draw out the letters again, copying them from a magazine he found in the cupboard. 'M I S S I N G.' Underneath, he writes, 'Cassie Paige, Age 7.'

He copies it out three more times, putting his face close to the page and holding his tongue between his teeth. He puts down the biro and clenches and unclenches his hand, holding it at the wrist. He pushes his arms out flat on the table, knocking a pile of papers off the other end, and lays his head on them for a moment. He sits like that for twenty minutes, thinking about Cassie, not noticing the moments slip out from under him.

Christopher stands up, reaches up to the radio on the ledge and turns it on.

'No news?' he says, as the radio presenter reels off the headlines.

When Christopher next opens his eyes, the clock on the wall reads 3.15 am.

His heart starts to race, and his arms tickle with pinpricks of sweat. When he closes his eyes, he can see her before him. She is wearing a yellow t-shirt and her hair is tied back with a pink hair band. She is cycling towards him, and it is summer.

He shivers in the chill air of the caravan. He gathers the

posters in front of him and stands up to pull on his waxed jacket.

He rummages in the cupboard under the kitchen sink for some string and a pair of scissors, which he shoves into his coat pocket before kicking open the caravan door.

He walks down the long garden, shining his flashlight before him. The church is a black shadow against the darkness of the night, and he keeps looking over his shoulder as if someone is there.

He squats down on the gravel and lays his torch on the ground so that its beam shines across the ground, the light thinning and spreading as it nears the church door. He makes holes in the paper with the end of the scissors and loops the string through, then lashes the poster onto the corner of the notice board.

'There,' he whispers to himself, 'that should hold 'til morning.'

He walks past the village shop and sees a pile of newspapers perched on the doorstep for the morning. He carries on walking until he gets to Long Road, where Cassie's family lives. He ties a poster to a lamppost.

'They'll feel better seeing that,' he says. 'They'll know we're thinking of them.'

Christopher thinks with detail about where to put each poster and, when he is down to two, he remembers he hasn't put one up on the notice board outside the shop. When he gets there, he can already see one of his posters attached to it. He is puzzled but puts it down to his tiredness.

'I shall have to do some more tomorrow night,' he says, 'there aren't enough.'

He ties the last one to the noticeboard outside the school.

He walks back to Alice's. She'll leave the door open for

him, she said, so he always knows he has somewhere to go. He isn't sure where he lives just now. In the in-between. The caravan, his Mum's house, Alice's.

There is a quiet humming and Christopher looks up to see the milk float making its way towards him.

'What on earth have you been up to?' the milkman shouts, as he pulls up alongside Christopher.

'Couldn't sleep with all that's happening,' Christopher mumbles as he trudges on, not looking up.

He rattles the door handle at Alice's but it is locked, so he goes back to the caravan and sleeps until midday.

When he wakes, Christopher makes himself a cup of tea. He smells the milk but decides against it. It's been sat out for two days.

A spider lowers itself from the window ledge and climbs back up again. Its small black body glows golden in the sunlight.

'I'll go out walking again,' he says to himself.

As he walks past the end of Cassie's road on the way to the Five Bells, he notices that the poster has been ripped down, leaving the white string wrapped around the post and little white flecks of paper along it, like sheep's fleece caught in a barbed wire fence.

'I'm only trying to help,' he says to himself, shrugging, as he walks up the two stone steps that lead to the pub. He goes straight up to the bar and asks if anyone has said anything about Cassie. The barman shakes his head.

'No, Christopher, they haven't. You have got to stop doing this. Let sleeping dogs lie and all that.'

He whispers with an urgent hiss, low and close to Christopher's face, then shakes his head as he wipes down the bar with a cloth.

'I can't,' Christopher says, and the barman turns away

with a wave of his hand. 'No news then,' Christopher says quietly into his pint.

It is still light when he leaves the pub, but the day is over again, already. The trail of land workers trudges slowly past him to the pub for their knocking-off pint.

Christopher sets off to walk around the village, faster now, because he needs answers. He is anxious about her, about where she could be, and starts to bite the nails on his left hand as he marches up Long Road. He peers into each house as he passes it. A family sit down to dinner: meat with peas and carrots. An old man and woman play cards.

He runs clumsily down the road in his loose work boots, calling her name into dykes, empty fields and cluttered-up barns.

We can't tell him; we have no voice. Only the ones who are living can do that. They can tell him, but they fear the rage when he finds out, and the come-down when he remembers. They'd rather let him pretend, if it hurts no one else. Like you would with a child. We can only hold him in our palms as his feet clatter along the roads. He'll come back around to the facts in the end. He always does.

A streetlight has spilt an orange glow on the pavement, but he steps out of its pool of light and carries on into the dark. He takes the shortcut rather than the main road, and he turns left along the curved lane which runs past the farm.

He is comfortable in the dark on these roads that he knows so well, but still, the wind urges him to walk quickly. As it whips across the quiet fields, he hunches up his shoulders and rams his fists down into his pockets. He can just about make out the curve of the road, by the dull glint of the moon reflecting on a car windscreen. A cat steps across his path. His eyes begin to turn glassy, welling up with sadness and drunkenness.

He stops walking, then. He just stops and breathes.

In. And out again.

He sways slightly. He can't hear a thing but the sweep of the wind and the rustle of bushes in the gardens about him.

Then, at once, the tears come, pulsing through his body with a force that shocks him. He finds himself on his hands and knees on the tarmac, stifling his sobs in case they wake someone. He can't believe he has let himself sit there drinking one, two, three pints, not knowing where she is. He pictures her shivering out in the cold somewhere. He pictures worse; her hurt and scared, the fresh shock of blood on her and shakes his head as he whispers, 'No, no, no.'

He starts to run back to Long Road. He runs messily and drunkenly until he stands before the tight row of houses, panting. In the first house, the lights are all off, except for one, and it shines like a beacon across the road and towards the fields beyond it. The window throws its light onto Christopher, who is shocked at his sudden illumination. A man watches a late-night movie.

After ten minutes of staring into the warm glow, he runs again. It is Alice's door that he finally collapses at, whimpering like a hurt dog. He bangs on it frantically and she appears, sleep in her eyes.

'What's wrong, Chris?' she says, as she hauls him over the step into the kitchen.

'It's Cassie,' he whispers. 'I can't find her. I've tried. I can't.'

He is curled in the doorway, heavy with the weight of himself. His shirt hangs loosely on his frame, and his shoes are caked in mud.

The voices swirl around his head but Cassie blazes from his heart.

He looks up at Alice and she starts shaking her head, but not in an angry way.

'Oh, Chris,' she says.

She helps him to his feet and steadies him as they go through to the lounge.

She fetches him a blanket and a cup of tea.

'Chris, I haven't seen you for two days.'

'I was at the caravan. I forgot it had been so long. I miss her.'

'I know you do. How about I fetch you some food and run you a bath?'

He nods, calmly.

His body has called him to his senses; it must have. He is cold and hungry. His body knows that he needs to rest. It betrays him, sometimes, cutting across the whirling of his mind with the simplest of things that it knows he needs: food, water, rest.

19

ALICE

ugust 2005

WHEN WE CLEAR his mother's house, Chris takes just a few things. He isn't bothered by the wardrobes full of clothes, the books that he'd had as a child, the love notes sent between his mother and father when they were courting. He takes his mum's turquoise address book. He shows me how you slide the marker down to the letter that you want and then press the button at the bottom so that it springs open, as if by magic, upon the letter you had chosen. He takes one of his father's pipes too, which still smells of tobacco. The mouthpiece is marked all around with dents from his father's teeth. He takes a blue tin sports car too, one of his or Ben's, I assume, a leftover relic from childhood. A photo, bleached out by the sun. Him and a girl, standing on the road. Her, not quite standing straight. Their sheepish grins. Proof that she lived.

These things he has gathered from his life; the essence of it distilled with such clarity. I realise he had lived like a ghost there, not making a mark or a fuss, always slipping into the background. And even now in my mother's house, my house I should say, with just the two of us, he's the same. It's as if he is trying to make himself invisible. He has hardly anything of his own. He lives like a fugitive among my things, hiding himself in my life.

The caravan is still perched in the undergrowth as it was. I dread what we'll find, it having been closed up for so long. The door squeaks as I open it and the stench of rotten milk and beer pours out. I flick the light switch, unthinking. It has been disconnected from the power supply.

A row of squeezed-out teabags sits along the edge of the counter, furring with mould. A pile of mud has accumulated on the doormat and the floor is littered with multicoloured crisp packets and chocolate bar wrappers. There are stacks of old newspapers. There is a box of small elastic bands that have spilled amber circles across the table. They would have been used for bunching the flowers, which Christopher hasn't done in years. On the desk, headed notepaper from his father's business and beer cans, pushed to the window and stacked one on top of the other. On the floor and in the cupboards too, more empty beer cans. I stand there dizzied by the smell.

'Is there anything you need, Chris?' I ask.

He looks around, and shakes his head, looking at it all.

He dismisses it with a wave of his hand and turns to go.

'You sure?' I call, as he marches furiously away.

He hunches in the bushes, brooding over all he has lost. I give him space, edging around him; not knowing what will trigger him.

The old house stands quietly empty each day. It's nearly

six months now since Marjorie died. The land has been sold for development. It will be demolished as it's no longer structurally sound, but it's hard for Christopher. He forgets, all the time.

Strange to think that all those years the house has stood there it could have crumbled around her. It was only after she'd died that they said it had to come down. It'll be better for Chris when it's gone; less to remind him of what had gone before.

His little kingdom is being dismantled, bit by bit, and I wonder what will remain when it has all gone. Will he see things clearly for once?

Today, we walk past, and the roof has gone. I picture Christopher and Ben lying in their beds, looking up at the sky. Christopher thinks this is funny, which I'm glad about. He walks around to the back although it is no longer his land. The large window stretches across the width of the flat-roofed extension. He ducks under the red and white striped tape that says, 'KEEP OUT' and goes up to the window. He peers in, his nose pressed flat to the cold glass, his curly greying hair flying away from his head. His eyes dart furiously from one corner of the kitchen, where the lino is peeling up in the corner, to the other, where the electric wires that were once attached to the cooker sprout like roots from the earth. He looks through into the dark lounge, where there are only two small windows to give light. There is a faded patch of carpet where so many feet have stepped down from the kitchen into the lounge.

'Why hasn't Mum made a fire today, Alice?'

I take a breath. Something has nudged him sideways into his other reality.

'Chris, she died, don't you remember? You found her in

the kitchen, didn't you? She's not here anymore. You live with me now.'

Chris looks at me intently, nodding slowly when he understands. It's like he slips back into his old world sometimes and has to be jolted back into this one, this crueller and spikier one. Which is why I need to be here, holding his hand, making him stay in the real one.

He vanishes some evenings, slipping out while I am tidying or in the bath, and I wait for him, worrying about what he is doing, imagining the worst. I wonder if he is getting worse.

Ben comes to visit more often; driven I think by guilt and curiosity. There is a distance between them still, between older and younger brother.

When Ben arrives today for the weekend, Christopher isn't here. He's gone off wandering, so I welcome Ben in and we wait. It feels strange to be here with just Ben, who has the same eyes as my Christopher but is so different. Chris comes home by lunchtime, and we head out to the Wash afterwards.

Christopher walks ahead, hacking at some weeds with a long stick, while I quickly spout out everything to Ben.

'Look, I know what it looks like, but he had to go somewhere after the caravan.'

'What does it look like?'

'I don't know what it looks like. Look, I don't know why I'm trying to justify myself to you, I don't even really know you. But Chris lives here now. I can support him better that way.'

I can see the questions fizzing through his mind.

'I sometimes wonder if my life is a path that has been decided for me because this isn't the path I would have chosen,'

I carry on, over-speaking, as always. 'But it isn't a bad path. Our lives are simple. We have our tea and toast rituals, our walks on Sundays, a beer in the pub every now and then. Because that is what all of this is about, isn't it? The little things?'

'I don't get why you're doing it. What's in it for you?'

'I don't know. It's not like that. All I know is that it has been laid in front of me and there is no way that I can say no.'

He tells me about his job as an English teacher and I tell him about my life as an artist, all the things I have done, all the time spent dreaming. And about how now that I am here, I have everything I want: a house, these skies, time to paint.

'So, it's all worked out pretty well for you,' he says.

'Yeah. Yes, it has, I suppose,' I say, realising he's leading me into a trap.

LATER THAT NIGHT, the back door opens with a bang and there is Christopher. He carries a dying robin that he found on the roadside.

'It must've been hit by a car,' he says.

The robin's chest flutters, and it fixes my gaze with its beady eye.

'I'll just put it on the woodshed,' says Christopher.

I sigh and Ben catches my eye. It is one of Christopher's triggers: anything on the roadside, anything dying. He works himself up and ends up pacing the garden, wondering what he can do to help. I hold his hands by his sides and his eyes dart furiously.

'There's nothing you can do to help that poor robin,' I say. 'The best we can do is leave it in the fresh air to get better. It's not your fault.'

I look him straight in the eyes and hope it gets through to him.

LATER THAT NIGHT, Chris is out wandering again. Ben and I are sitting in the half-dark, talking. I am gathering clues.

'So, what happened with Cassie? Christopher told me she went missing, but what happened? Were there any leads? Was she abducted?'

Ben looks at me, drops his head to his hands and lets out some kind of a moan. He looks up again.

'He didn't tell you that?'

I nod.

'She didn't go missing, Alice. She was killed, hit by a car just outside the village shop. They were seven. Christopher saw the whole thing.'

20

ALICE

September 2005

SOME DAYS IT GOES AWAY; he is quiet, and life is okay. We walk together, we paint up in my studio, he goes off wandering.

I'm painting my way through Leo's diary. It's like a jigsaw puzzle. I can match the feeling to the colours in the sky. Today I pick out this quote:

IT IS A SWEET DAY, quiet with almost no sound. So different this place can be, summer to winter, spring to autumn, and I marvel at it. Today is a kind day, the kind where the earth rises up and blesses you, just because it can.

· · ·

THE SKY IS a strong bright blue. No clouds.

This morning, he isn't in the house when I wake. It's not unusual for him to not be here. But when I go outside to put the bin out after breakfast, there are all these dead animals lined up outside the back door. I wonder where he found them all, injured like that all at once. I count eleven of them: three birds, four shrews, two rabbits with broken necks, a badger, a mole.

I leave them there, thinking Christopher will come back soon and we'll talk it through and make it make sense for him again. I don't think much of it until lunch when he still hasn't come home.

I busy myself finishing off the canvas, but he hasn't come home by nightfall, so I take a torch out walking with only the moon for company. I tell myself not to panic because he has done this so many times, because he is an adult, because I'm not his carer, just his friend, but sometimes I feel I don't know what he's truly capable of.

I go straight to his mother's house, which is only a pile of rubble now. The sheds are gone, along with his childhood garden. He wasn't here to see it.

I SNEAK under the tape and walk around the demolition site, calling his name. The brambles have been cleared all along the ditch, and it looks bare.

I walk back towards the road with my torch flashing over the bushes at the front of the property. He is sitting there on the ground, his hunched form visible by moonlight.

'Chris! There you are! Come home! I've been looking everywhere for you.'

'But I need to wait for Cassie because she won't know

where to go,' he says intently. 'It's okay, she's coming back and I'm waiting for her.'

'But Chris, she isn't coming back.'

I know this now, but I can't reason with him. There is nothing I can say to dissuade him. He won't leave in case she comes back. I walk away in tears, helpless. I come back with food and sleeping bags and stay with him. I don't know what else to do.

We sit up for two days straight.

He is wired, rocking back and forwards all night. In the morning, he is pasty white, his red, dull eyes squinting in the sunlight.

Even I feel like I'm going insane.

'She isn't coming back, Chris. I think we need to get you some help.'

I ring Ben at 6 am.

'What do I do?' I say, pacing the pavement outside what used to be their family home. 'He won't leave. He says Cassie is coming back. He's like a giant fucking dog that won't move. How do you move a giant fucking dog?'

'Food?' Ben says half-joking.

'I'm so tired, I can't think. I'm going mad. I swear we're both going mad. What should I do, Ben? Tell me what to do.'

'I think you need to ring the police. Do you want me to come over?'

'I don't know,' I say, then hang up.

Trembling, I call 999.

'What service do you need?'

'Er, I don't know. Police? My friend is losing his mind. He won't eat or move from where he is sitting. He's been here for two days. He's sat up two nights straight. Can you help me?' I sob.

'Ok love,' she says. 'Don't worry. I'm going to put you through to emergency psychiatric care and they'll be able to help you, ok?'

I nod even though she can't see me.

I sit out by the privet hedge on the main road, not caring about the attention when the villagers start wandering up the road for the morning paper. The emergency services come within an hour; two big burly men, wearing dark green paramedic clothing. They smile at me.

'He's around the back,' I say. 'There's nothing more I can do for him; he won't reason with me. He's lost himself.'

They are strong and they gently pull him up to standing. He doesn't even put up a fight.

But the way he looks at me when they pull him to his feet, as if I've broken his trust, as if I've broken everything.

'Just a few days,' one of the men says to him. 'It will help you make sense of everything.'

When they link their arms through his and lead him down the garden path, he goes quietly. But as they close the ambulance doors, he calls out a name. It's not mine. It is Cassie's.

In the quiet, after they have gone, I gather up his dirty collection of belongings: the sleeping bag, his packet of cookies and his torch. I kick the two dead birds into a bush. The tears are streaming down my face because I am doing everything that I can for him, and it still isn't enough. He isn't even mine. Why do I care so much for him, this over-grown child? Because I love him? Yes, I love him.

When I get home, I pitch the row of dead animals into the ditch with a growing fury and I lock myself in the bath-room and sink onto the chequered tiles, my back against the door. I cry until I am exhausted. Then I just wait there, listening to the quietness of the house. I can hear the wind blowing outside.

What now, I think, in the calm. What now? Why am I spending my life picking up the pieces of his continual breakdown? And I can see the tunnel of my life getting smaller and darker before me, with no hope of a way out.

21

———

CHRISTOPHER

September 2005

ALICE SAID it would do me good that I was to wait here until she came back for me but she ain't coming it's been a long time what if Cassie comes and I am not there? what if she's been waiting all this time in the bushes, yes that's right, waiting all the time I am sure of it what if there was something I have forgot, something that she needed to tell me? we are best friends you see best friends until the end of the earth so how could she have gone? it don't happen like that there must be something I am forgetting that's why I try to remember I go over it and over it but my mind won't set it straight I can't find the list that Mum left me she said she'd leave one for how to make it right again but now she's gone too a nice lady here says just take the pills and dream but when I close my eyes I think of Cass and that makes me feel worse than ever the walls are white but spiders crawl on them and the voice keeps calling the ceilings so high it makes me cold I want Alice to take me home now because I can't remember it right best friends don't keep no secrets there must be something I'm forgetting I'll wait until Alice comes I'll wait, and then we'll sort out what to do Alice always knows what to do take me home

22

—————

ALICE

September 2005

CHRISTOPHER IS AWAY for two weeks. He is sedated at the ward and mostly sleeps, they tell me. I call every day to find out how he is doing. They give him anti-depressants and sedatives, a whole cocktail. He is distressed and asks after me, but I don't visit. I can't. I sleep, wake, sleep, wake. I can't paint. I can't think.

Ben comes to stay with me one weekend while he goes to visit Christopher. When Ben gets back that evening, I'm sitting in the armchair clutching a cold cup of tea and I can't remember how long I have been there.

'He'll be okay; he's coming through it,' he says.

But I won't be okay, will I? I feel like saying. No one thinks about how I will be. Well, they do. They warned me, didn't they? Warned me that nothing has worked before, that nothing could ease the trauma from his mind. But admitting that I need help is admitting failure. And then, I realise that I am nursing again, just like before. He is unfixable, just like those others were.

After Ben leaves, I pack my bags to go to Cambridge. Christopher won't know that I'm gone. I need something for me, some dialogue on my level, some comfort for myself.

For some reason, I turn up at Pete's house. It has been four months since I've seen him. He isn't there; I assume he must be at work, so I walk along the river in the fog of a cold September afternoon.

I am sitting on his step when he gets back from work.

'My God, Alice. How long have you been there?'

'Not long.'

He embraces me and I wonder if I could love him again. Truth is, I am desperate for love, any kind of love.

'What are you doing here?'

'Just wondered how you've been.'

He shrugs.

'I'm ok. Gave up the creative thing, job in an office now. All sold out.'

'But you can pay the bills at least?

'Well, yeah, there's that.'

'The creative life isn't all it's cracked up to be, is it? Can I come in?'

He shifts awkwardly.

'Alice, I'm happy to have a chat but, you know, things have moved on; I've met someone.'

I wonder if my smile falters.

'Oh, wow. Is she here?'

'Well, yeah, we live together.'

'Oh, I'll go,' I say, fumbling for my car keys in my handbag. 'I don't know what I was thinking. Sorry.'

I turn and start to walk away up the street, but Pete runs after me and takes hold of my hand.

'Look, Al, how long are you here? Do you fancy getting a coffee sometime?'

'No, no, don't worry about it. See you around, yeah?' I say, tears pinching at my eyes. I am such an idiot.

I walk off quickly, my cheeks flushed with shame. Who am I to think I can turn up in his life again after it fell apart the first time? But what now, I wonder, as I hurry away, my vision blurring with tears.

I walk back to the car, trying to remember what I came back for. It was for some idea of comfort, something that I can't find up there in the black night of the village. Something that my loneliness has been telling me I had down here. But the truth is, it's not here either.

I can't stop the tears. I turn up at Sophie and Nick's and knock on the door.

'Alice!' she exclaims loudly when she sees me. 'What the hell? Where's Chris?'

I collapse onto her shoulder.

'Chris has been taken into a psychiatric ward,' I explain. 'I called the police; I didn't know what to do. He sat outside his mother's house for two days straight, thinking that Cassie was coming back again.'

She leads me into the flat and I collapse onto the sofa.

'Who is this Cassie and why does she have such a hold over him?'

'She died in a car crash. She's his best friend. He thinks she's just gone missing. He thinks she's coming back again.'

'And he's never got over it. He won't accept that she's really gone.'

I nod.

'He told me she'd gone missing. I believed him for

months. I didn't find out what really happened until Ben told me a few weeks ago. I thought Christopher had his head screwed on after what he told me about Leo, but he really believes she's coming back. He was just sat there, waiting. I didn't know what to do for him, so I rang the police.'

Thankfully, wherever Sophie is, there is good food. A beef stew is bubbling on the stove, and I don't know how she did it when she didn't know I was coming, but the smell of it feels like home. It feels like love. Nick brings me a cup of tea. I smile, gratefully.

'He's fine. He's sedated, but he'll come through it. So I just got in the car and drove. I didn't really think too much about it. And then I turned up at Pete's. You didn't tell me he had a new girlfriend.'

Sophie and Nick look at each other.

'He doesn't have a new girlfriend.'

I look at them blankly.

'Alice, he loves you. Has done all along. He was too scared to come after you.'

'He just told me he lives with someone!'

'Maybe he's trying to protect himself?' Nick offers vaguely.

'From what? Why didn't he come over? I only moved away to see if he really loved me. Well, that's not the only reason, but he could have come to find me.'

'But you called it a day when you left.'

'Well, whatever, I just practically offered myself to him and he didn't want to know.'

Sophie and Nick look at each other again.

'What? Guys, I'm so tired of being an adult. Tired of being a carer to a man who doesn't know how to live and can't fix his past. This tea is nice and all, but is there any wine?'

'There is always wine,' says Sophie, and I thank God that she answered the door and that, of all the places in the world, I am here.

We talk until late and drink all the wine in the house until I curl up on the sofa and sleep like a baby.

In the morning, I feel wretched, hungover and embarrassed. I'm a 38-year-old woman getting drunk on heartbreak.

Sophie brings me a latte and a croissant.

'Al. It's great to see you. You're always welcome here, hell or high water. Tell me you know that.'

I nod, sheepishly.

The doorbell rings. I can hear Pete's voice talking to Nick. I am still on the sofa, wrapped in the heavy duvet. Part of me wants to spring into action, sort out my hair and my smudged make-up and throw on some clothes, but then I decide it's not going to happen.

He puts his head around the door to the lounge.

'Look, Al, do you want to meet later to talk?'

'Later, later,' I mumble.

An hour later, when I have eaten a little, showered and dressed, I meet Pete in a café that's aiming for the fifties' diner vibe, all black leather booths and chequered table-cloths. We sit in the window watching the streams of people walk by. My head is still pounding even though I took a couple of paracetamols half an hour ago.

'Black americano please,' I say to the waitress.

'Anything to eat?' Pete asks.

'No, no. Still feeling a bit tender.'

'I'll have a latte please,' he says, passing back the menu to the waitress.

'So, Al. Why are you here? What's going on?'

'I've just had enough of being a grown-up. Is that okay?'

'I haven't got a girlfriend.'

'I know. Nick and Soph told me that much.'

'They don't know everything about me.'

'Yeah, they do,' I say with a smile.

'Well, yeah, okay,' he agrees with a laugh. 'I wasn't expecting to see you. I panicked.'

'I should have warned you. It's just that things aren't going so well up there and I had to get out. Sometimes, it comes over me like a fog and I just have to get away. It's not just the village; it's Christopher. I'm stuck in this thing that I can't get out of.'

'Christopher's the guy with the problems?'

I nod. 'I guess Soph filled you in. It's like he can't grow up. His best friend died in an accident, and he can't get past it. He waits for her all the time; he thinks she's coming back for him. He goes around in circles.'

'So how did you get out?' he asks.

'He's in a psych ward. And I didn't do it just to get a week off,' I laugh weakly. 'He was sitting on his mother's land, where his house used to be, and he wouldn't leave in case Cassie came back. I didn't know what to do with him, so I called the police after two days.'

'But he's not even your family. Why have you given everything up for him? Are you... you know?'

'What, together? No, no. I'm more like a big sister, or a mother, or a carer, I dunno. We're mates, I guess.' I shrug.

'So, what's in it for you?' Pete asks, staring straight at me.

That's what everyone has been asking. The more they ask it, the more I wonder what in the hell I am actually doing it for.

'Things aren't that clear cut, are they?' I reply curtly. 'His mother asked me to keep an eye on him a week before she died, and now I'm involved and it feels too late to step out. He has a brother, Ben, but he lives miles away. Ben's got young children; I don't think they'd cope with him.'

'You're not coping with him! And Al, it's not your responsibility!'

'So whose is it? No, I'm not coping, but I can't see a way out. Anyway, how are you?'

'You need to change something, Al, I'm not going to let you go under for some guy's dead mother who asked you to watch out for him. He needs help. And you need to stop letting guilt control your life. You haven't changed.'

'He's getting help,' I say, but I think, <u>Tosser</u>. He's completely right. I know it but I'm too proud to be corrected. Why do things seem so obvious from the outside?

'So how are things?' I ask.

'So so; happy enough, I suppose.'

'I don't believe you.'

'What do you want me to say, that I've missed you since the day you left?' he says, looking at me with his deep brown eyes.

'Well, have you? I mean, why didn't you come and see me?'

'Because you left. And that told me you were finished with me.'

'But you didn't even text, you didn't call. If it meant so much to you, why didn't you try to save it? Us, I mean.'

'You didn't call me either. My pride is easily wounded. What can I say?'

I suppose what he says is fair enough but it still fills me with uncertainty; a feeling that I don't understand like a rip tide pulling my feet from under me. And right now, I don't think I have the strength to swim against it.

We leave the café and walk around the city, and he shows me what has changed. Not all that much, it seems. One of the pubs we used to go to is boarded up, but mostly what has changed in the last six months is me.

I have become disconnected, like Christopher. I have cut myself off from everything I used to know. I left Cambridge to focus on my art, and I've fallen into this trap of caring. I'm giving my life to the care of this man, who takes everything from me with no thanks at all, just like a child.

Pete and I spend the day together, talking about everything, filling each other in on the past few months.

Soph texts me at midnight. 'Not coming home?'

'Not,' I reply.

At his flat, Pete pours me a glass of white wine. I am determined to keep drinking so I don't think through what I am about to do. He comes to sit next to me on the sofa, says, 'I've missed you so much, Al,' and the tears seep out of the corners of my eyes because of everything – everything that is too much for me to hold. He kisses me and it feels normal and it feels like home.

We spend the night together. I feel like a teenager again, freed from the weight of responsibility. When I leave his the next morning, it is with a full heart; one of sadness to be leaving, but one that has been brought back to life. It reminds me again that all sorts of lives are possible. It reminds me that even I am worthy of love.

23

ALICE

September 2005

BEFORE THE HOSPITAL DISCHARGES HIM, Christopher, Ben and I have a meeting with his psychiatrist, Dr Michael Skinner. He seems nice enough. He wears a grey suit, and his white hair is cut neatly to his head. We meet in a room with white flocked wallpaper and high ceilings.

'I believe you are still reliving the trauma of losing your best friend,' he says to Christopher, 'so we need a way to diffuse the power that your memories have over your emotions.'

Chris nods.

'It was tragic for you as a child that your friend went missing. I think it has triggered a form of schizoaffective disorder. You were obviously deeply attached to her.'

'She didn't go missing,' Ben says quietly. 'She was killed in an accident.'

Dr Skinner looks over his glasses at Ben.

'Sorry, what was that?'

Christopher is looking at the ceiling, and humming.

'She's dead. Now you understand why she has such a hold on him. It was late Summer, just before the return to school, the apples ready, the harvest coming in. August is always hard for him.

WE ALL BECOME aware of Chris for a second. He is standing now, moving slowly around the room, touching the walls – gently stroking them – and humming under his breath.

Dr Skinner turns to me, as the carer.

'This isn't in his notes,' he says.

'He told me she went missing. I believed him until Ben told me two weeks ago.'

Dr Skinner looks between us, at a loss. I feel shame for not having known the truth. Stupidity. Why didn't Ben tell me earlier? He thought I knew, that's why. I think back to the first time we talked in my mother's kitchen.

Dr Skinner takes a breath.

'This loss affects him deeply. He carries it still. Cassie's death has triggered some sort of trauma response that has negatively impacted Christopher's ability to live an independent life.'

He pauses for a moment and looks up at Christopher.

'I think it will be helpful to talk about her more; to get it all out no matter how tiring, and exhaust the memories. Christopher,' he says, realising that he isn't addressing his patient. 'Look at pictures of her, maybe even write down all of your memories. Because at least then they will be on the outside and not on the inside. How do you feel about that?'

I am reticent, knowing what a shadow she already casts over our lives.

Christopher is still humming and pressing his face up close to a replica of Degas' *Dancer, Tilting*.

He wafts his hand behind him as if to dismiss Dr Skinner.

'I worry that it will bring her to the fore more than she already is,' I confess in a low voice, and I can see us drowning in a whirlpool of self-pity.

'Will you trust me on this one and just have a go until next time, and then we'll see where we're up to? Take Chris' lead. If he wants to talk about her, go with it. Be led by him.'

I smile weakly. He turns back to Chris.

'Have a seat, Christopher,' he says, 'I know a lot of Fen people don't like to talk, it's not in their character somehow. But I believe it's the only way you can get past this. The more you talk, the more these memories will lessen their grip on you.'

Christopher nods.

I wonder how much he understands of this.

IN THE CAR on the way home, I say, 'Chris, I'm sorry that Cassie died. That must have been awful for you.'

I need it to be real. I need him to say that it is real.

But he just looks out of the window at the fields, the houses, the cows. The silence hangs between us.

Sometimes I could scream or bang his head against a window. But everything is supposed to be normal and calm, so I swallow it down and grab the steering wheel tighter.

. . .

Just as quietly as he went, Christopher is home and slips back into things. He isn't angry with me like I thought he might be. He doesn't blame me for ringing the police. He doesn't blame me for not visiting. I think it's a blur for him.

But a few weeks in, after he is used to the new medication, after Ben has gone home and after he has been out walking one night, he bursts in through the back door and says, 'I don't know if I can take any more,' and it feels like our lives are going around in circles.

He looks down at his fingers, which are red raw from his anxious gnawing. He lingers in the doorway to the living room.

'Of what?' I ask, one eye still on the television, the other aware of his presence in the doorway.

In the orange light from the kitchen, he casts a shadow across the wooden floor. I watch the glitzy dancers spin around and around on the screen.

It is not the first time I've heard this. To be honest, I am tired of it. Everything is too much for him.

'Of it all,' he says.

I keep my eyes fixed on the dancers. I try not to roll them or close them or even exhale loudly. Finally, I turn towards him. He looks at me intently, ready to hang on my every word.

'It's this again, is it?' I ask.

His hands are pushed into the pockets of his dirty jeans. The slump of his shoulders is like a down-turned smile.

I press the switch on the television and watch as the picture vanishes. I push myself up from the chair and walk towards him, put my arms around him and push his weight back against the doorframe.

'Oh, Chris.'

My ear against his chest, I listen to his beating heart. Its continuous thump reassures me somehow. He has put on extra weight since his mum died, and it makes me want to cry. There is so much of him outside and yet, inside, so little to hold on to.

'What happened?' I say, into the wool of his jumper.

It smells of smoke mingled with sweat, but still, I breathe it in deeply. The way that he smells reassures me; he is too substantial to be erased. It is always at the end of the night when he unravels. I wonder how I can pull him back together, and think of the joke, 'Doctor, Doctor, I feel like a pair of curtains.' I smile to myself.

He pushes me away from him and holds me by the wrists at arm's length. He looks straight at me, his grey eyes full of the sea.

'It's nothing,' he says. 'I was just thinking.'

But he is coming undone the way stuffing spills from the burst seam of a toy. I can see it.

I ask what else he is looking for and he spreads his hands out, palms upwards, like a child, as if waiting to catch the answer.

'Chris. I don't know how I can help,' I say.

'I just miss her.'

'I know you do, Chris.'

'And,' he pauses. 'Sometimes I don't know if I can go on without her.'

She hovers around our lives, just on the edge. Always there.

I know it will make things worse to cry and I pinch my eyelids closed but I am too tired, and the salt lines trace their way down to my chin. How can I answer? How can I be her when I am not her? How can I be what he needs when it is something I am not?

'Tell me about her,' I say, and his eyes light up.

I make us sweet tea and toast and we sit on the two wingback chairs that face each other in the sitting room. I say, 'Tell me everything.'

He looks at me, unsure, and I nod for him to continue.

'There was this time when we found a hedgehog in the graveyard. We wrapped him in a blanket and took it to Mrs Paige, Cassie's mum. She turfed us out with some pennies to get cat food. We fed him under the hedge in her garden, only because that's where his home was. He had a meal and then went, and we didn't see him again. But that was a long time ago, wasn't it Alice? She wouldn't do that now, would she? Cassie wouldn't.'

'What else?'

'Her Dad was a mechanic, always fixing cars. We were best friends. But she was always a tomboy. They moved away, after the bad thing.'

There, he admits it. He relives his friendship with her like it is all right here, like he has to stay seven forever so that when she gets back, they will be the same age again. He can't get past his obsession with her, his long-gone girl.

'One time, we were in the willow, and she was sad. Her dad had smacked her for getting mud on the carpet. Ever so strict they were. She could never be quite good enough for them, it seemed. I cuddled her, told her I'd always look after her. Couldn't though, could I? Couldn't keep her safe.'

When he is talked out, he goes up to his bedroom, and I stand there in the quiet. A void descends like fog between us sometimes. I can't reach him because it is him and her, and nothing else matters. There are walls as thick as rooms between us. I realise how lonely I am, living with him.

Who is there that will listen to me, that will ask me what I care about, what I love? I think about Pete and that night and how good it felt to be heard, to be touched, to be held.

But he hasn't called me since and I haven't called him. What was it for then? Something we both wanted for a moment but that we both know is not the right thing. When will I start making wise decisions, I wonder.

I go up to Chris' bedroom and sit for a while holding his hand. He has already fallen asleep. I can't help crying, for some reason.

After a while, I stop and feel calmer for it, washed out. I listen to the steady rhythm of his breathing. In. Out. In. Out. I change my breathing to keep time with his. I take comfort in the fact that at least when he sleeps, he is at peace.

THE NEXT DAY, I wake him with a cup of tea.

'I've been thinking,' I say. 'We need to make the book like Dr Skinner said.'

He nods. 'That sounds good.'

'How about a walk out on the Wash first though? It's a beautiful day.'

He looks uncertain and sits on the edge of the bed worrying about it, his fingers pressed together. Sometimes he can't bear to leave the house; sometimes he won't stay in. I don't think he knows what he wants half of the time. I sure as hell don't, that's what makes it so hard.

'Come on,' I say, gently pushing his shoulder, 'the air at least will do us both good.'

After half an hour of persuading, we drive out there. It always makes me feel better to be out at the Wash; it puts things into perspective. When I haven't been for a while, I crave the emptiness of the skies, the wind and the way that the sun shines off the wet mud flats. The skinny white clouds have been drawn across the sky like pencil lines today, like tiny cracks in china. The light makes Chris' skin look grey. He is paler since the hospital.

I try not to let him see how much I look at him. We walk for a long time until our calves ache, but we hardly speak.

'You won't leave me, will you, like she did?' he says.

He doesn't look at me but towards the murky horizon. I smile and say what I want so badly to mean with all of myself.

'Of course not. Where else would I go?'

We keep walking and my heart tremors with the lie. He must know I am already thinking of running.

Behind us, a bird screeches as it dives towards the water, and the horizon blinks in the sunlight, unwavering, unending.

24

ALICE

September 2005

OVER THE NEXT FEW WEEKS, we make Cassie's book. Christopher tells me everything he can remember in long, disjointed stories and I try to work it into something chronological. He puts in sketches of her, her bike, her face, the day they first met Leo. Chris becomes obsessed with it, and I think it is kind of helpful too, so we go with it for now. Every time he remembers something new, he puts it in. I am amazed at how much he remembers. I wonder if this will somehow exhaust his pot of memories, leaving no fuel for his madness.

I go outside to hang the bedsheets up as it is a bright day with a light wind. A wave of nausea washes over me and I run to the hedge to retch. I have felt odd for a week or so and I wonder what it could be. And then I think back to that night six weeks ago with Pete and it makes my stomach lurch.

Pete hasn't made contact since I came back. It's the same old, same old, but here, with all these straight roads and empty skies, I feel snowed out in the wilds. It feels like a different world to Cambridge. Perhaps the gap is just too wide for Pete to cross. I wonder why I always make excuses in my mind for him. If he misses me, why doesn't he call me?

The next morning, I tell Christopher that we need to go into Wisbech to get some food. It is quiet on the roads, in the grey November light. The trees flash by on either side of the car, the emptiness of the fields spreading out all around us.

'What do we need, Christopher?' I ask, trying to distract myself.

'Tins of beans. Teabags. Cheese.'

'All good suggestions,' I say. 'What are we having tonight for dinner?'

'How about a nice beef pie?'

'Sounds good to me, shall we see if the butcher's got one ready?'

I slip a pregnancy test into the basket almost as an afterthought, and Chris doesn't notice.

Later, when we're back home, I lock myself in the bathroom and follow the instructions on the pack. I leave the test on the windowsill behind the toilet and look up at the flakes of paint coming away in the corner of the ceiling to pass the time.

And then I pick up the test and I know before I look. There are two strong lines. I read the instructions and look again and it's pretty clear. It says yes. I will have Pete's child.

'Shit,' I whisper, as my heart flips in my chest.

I go upstairs to my room and undress and stand looking at myself in the mirror. I don't know whether to believe it. I pat my belly and twist and turn; I look the same, so how can I suddenly be two people?

I come back downstairs and move about in a daze, while Christopher watches television. All sorts of questions throw themselves up in my mind. Will I tell Pete? When? Will he move up? What about the village, what will they think at the sight of me pregnant, sharing a house with Chris? Will I be able to live with Chris still? What about the baby? Will I carry it to term? Am I ready to care for a baby?

I don't have any of the answers, but one thing is for sure; I have been waiting for something unexpected to throw itself up in my life and here it is.

But how we will live, I don't know.

On and on my mind reels.

25

ALICE

O ctober 2005

THE MORE I think about it, the angrier I feel with Pete. What is it about women's choices that so define their lives? Why do our bodies have to bear evidence of our actions? I make one bad choice, or one good choice, who knows, and it will change the course of my life forever.

The baby grows and still, I have told no one. I don't want to be tied to Pete, do I? And what am I to do with Chris, while I sort out my life?

I ring Sophie one evening.

'Hi Soph, are you well?'

'Yes, great, good to hear your voice.'

'Soph, I really need to see you, but I don't know what I can do with Chris. Can you come up?'

'Well, it's pretty manic at the cafe but I'll try to find cover. What's going on?'

'I'd rather tell you in person,' I manage to get out.

'You sound like you need me.'

I nod and start to cry right there on the telephone.

'Yeah, I do,' I manage to whisper.

'Let me see what I can do. I'll text you.'

She comes up the next weekend. We pick her up at the station and when we are back home, we walk up the road and back, leaving Christopher at home watching a film. I'm pretty sure he won't go anywhere with Star Wars on.

'I'm pregnant,' I say, as soon as we are out of the house, 'and it's Pete's baby.'

She cannot prevent her jaw from dropping open.

'Are you sure?'

I nod. 'It's 13 weeks now. I'm so stupid.'

'You're not stupid.'

She hugs me. I can tell she doesn't know what to say.

'One time?'

'Yep. Ridiculous, isn't it?'

'I guess everything happens for a reason?' she says, unconvincingly.

I laugh. 'Does it, though? Isn't that just one of those things people say to make themselves feel better?'

She shrugs.

'Yeah. To be honest, I have no idea what to say. Are you going to keep it?'

'It's too late to do anything else. But it will change everything. I don't know what to do about Pete. Shall I tell him? He hasn't even called me. And what about Chris?'

'You could come down and talk to Pete.'

'But I can't leave Chris!'

'What about Ben? Next time he comes over, you could come and stay for a while.'

'I guess.'

'You need a break, Al. Honestly, I don't know how you've got yourself into this.'

She hugs me and I start to cry again. I wish she lived nearer.

THE NEXT MORNING, I am the first to wake. I go up to the studio and sit there on my painting stool, looking out to the world. Skeins of low mist cling to the furrows. Sugar beet lines the fields across from the house. The sunlight turns the clouds to silver and then gold as it slowly warms the earth.

I put my canvas up on the easel, take a swig of coffee and start off. The first brush of paint on the canvas is the boldest. I mix cadmium red and phthalo blue until I get the rich brown of the furrows. The sky is the palest blue, opaque, like fine porcelain. Titanium white mixed with the tiniest smear of ultramarine captures a touch of its frailty.

The clouds roll over the field; the fog is lit like dust across a room. Everything is held in the finest balance.

26

ALICE

Deccember 2005

BEN COMES to stay as soon as he breaks up for Christmas and I escape to Cambridge for a few days. I leave him comprehensive instructions for looking after Chris: his favourite foods, the things we like to do, how to cope if he has a flashback. It is hard to pack all that I know about Chris onto a note on two sides of A4.

The car is on the blink, so I take the train and am glad for the journey. I have always loved train rides; the way you are rocked like a baby. It feels, for the first time in a long time, like I am escaping. All the towns are strung with lights for Christmas, and everything feels okay, just for this moment. The thought comes to me that, deep down, I am amazed that I am bringing a life into the world. I never thought I would have the chance. And it is a grace perhaps, mixed in with it all. Will I be a good mother, I wonder, and I think back to Mum, and how I couldn't be what she needed.

I decide right there and then, I will have this baby and love this baby, whether Pete wants to be involved or not. A bubble of something rises up in me. Joy? A change coming? Or is it that there is something new and unsullied to come?

I have arranged to meet Pete after he finishes work for dinner at a little Italian place just around the corner from Soph and Nick's. He knows I have something to say. I arrive first and take my seat. The nerves creep up and I feel like I have betrayed him; I should have said something sooner. I feel sick.

He arrives and reaches down to kiss me on the cheek. I stand and the evidence is there between us.

'Oh my God, Alice, is this what you had to talk to me about?'

He looks angry.

Tears spring to my eyes and I nod. 'It's yours' I say, realising I wish it wasn't true.

He looks incredulous. 'From that one night?'

I nod.

'How can you be sure?'

'Well, I haven't slept with anyone else, if that's what you're asking. There was never a good time to tell you. I couldn't leave Chris. I'm sorry.'

'Are you sure you and Chris haven't got something going on?'

'I'm his carer, not his girlfriend!' I say, flustered, and sit down again.

I shouldn't have surprised him like this. It's not fair, he has no time to process. He reels.

'You know abortion is legal, don't you?' he says in a voice that is too loud for the quiet restaurant.

I look down. Stunned. 'Not anymore, it's not. I'm five months in already.'

'Fuck. It's a lot to take on, Al. Couldn't you have told me earlier? On the telephone?'

'I wanted to tell you face to face,' I say, then falter. Everything that I thought I'd say evaporates.

'How come you never came up to visit? After that night?'

He shrugs.

'What is it that keeps you here?'

'I like it here.'

'I just thought ... what if it's fate? What if we're meant to be together?' But even as I say it, I know I don't really believe it.

'Just because you say you're having my baby? I don't believe in fate.'

He shakes his head and I feel like an idiot. I can feel my cheeks flush.

'We're too different, Al, we want different things.'

'Do we? How do you know what I want?' I say in a quieter voice.

The waitress comes over and we order, though I don't feel like sitting in the same room as him anymore, this man that I have been thinking about for three months, stitching myself a life full of hope in my imagination.

I order meatballs and pasta, even though I still feel sick.

Where does this leave me? I wonder as we wait for the food. It dawns on me that it is of no consequence to him what I do.

Now that it is all out between us, it feels like there is nothing left to say. We eat awkwardly, trying to talk about other, more light-hearted things, but our unborn child rests between us and now everything is different.

Pete offers to pay, and I am relieved to stand up and get

away.

'So, that's it then,' I say, picking up my bag and moving towards the door. I don't even say bye. Sometimes it's better to just leave.

The night air is cool and it's what I need.

'I'm all on my own,' I find myself whispering.

I've told him it's his; I've done my part. There can be no good way to end it with everything that is between us. A whole lifetime of questions and imaginings, and he shuts the door on it, easy as anything.

I walk around to Soph and Nick's in a daze, still shocked by Pete's reaction. Maybe I expected too much of him. I suppose I've been getting used to the idea for months and he only had five minutes to adjust.

'He doesn't want to know,' I say as I crash down onto their sofa.

'He'll come around,' Sophie says, and then, with a hug, 'and if not, then you're better off without him.'

I know she is trying to be hopeful, but her words don't make me feel any better.

THE NEXT DAY, Soph takes me shopping. We walk around the streets of Cambridge, lit with Christmas lights, and I can't help but feel a little bit more alive and excited about things. I choose this child. I choose this baby. It will change my life and I am so ready for it.

As I sit on the train back to the village, the next day I realise that everything has changed. But I have a small and brave feeling that we will be okay.

'Just me and you then, babe,' I whisper to my swelling belly, tapping it lightly with my fingertips as I watch the houses flash by.

27

ALICE

May 2006

I HAVE BEEN TRYING to disguise it as best I can but, with the summer coming, I'm burning up with anything more than one layer on. People have been talking in the village. Lynn, who runs the village store, comes right up to me in the street. She stops dead in front of me and points her finger at my chest.

'That Christopher isn't up to fatherhood. It's a disgrace. You aren't even married and he's not all there. What would Marjorie say if she knew?'

I laugh out loud at her audacity.

'You don't know anything about me,' I say, incredulously, and breeze past her. I don't have to explain myself to anyone. I refuse to set her straight.

She bristles and carries on walking. Let them think what they want. The outspoken ones I can deal with, it's the other ones that get to me; the slow shakes of the head, the averted gazes.

I feel like I need a placard saying, 'It's not Christopher's baby.'

Over and over, I wonder what I was thinking that night with Pete. It doesn't matter to him; he doesn't have to wear it like I do. There are no implications for him. He can just carry on as if his life hasn't changed.

As the months go by, Christopher seems more stable. His new medication has taken the mania away and he is back to himself, mostly. We walk, we paint, we cook. It is a simple life, and we are okay. I hesitate to say it, but I think the scrapbook worked. Everything is out. It can't roll around his head in frustration because it is now outside of him. When he feels sad about her, he takes the book out again, reads it through and laughs at the stories. He touches the sun-bleached photograph, stroking her hair. He cries too, scribbling over the top with more and more memories of her.

I try to talk to Christopher about the baby.

'You know there's a change coming soon?'

'Is there Al?'

'You know I'm looking slightly different, and have been visiting the doctor? I'm having a baby, Chris.'

He snaps out of his reverie. 'A baby, Al?'

I nod, wondering how this is all going to go.

'Yes, Chris, A baby. It's going to change everything.'

He changes the subject then, and I have no idea if he realises what is about to happen.

While I have the time, I paint the day, but already the empty life I craved is slipping from me.

Leo's words this morning:

. . .

THE WINDOW IS tall and light floods in from over the fields. I watch a flock of birds take flight from a wire, all at once. They are a screech of noise, a black cloud forming and reforming. They fly off to another wire, spun between two pylons, which sags like a slack tightrope under their weight. The sky is pale with cold. It just feels further away, feels as if something has changed. I feel, coming here, as if I've given in.

He was talking about the winter that he moved in, and how he couldn't get used to being inside.

I paint the sky and the birds, jumpy on the wire, and they remind me of myself, of the butterflies in my stomach at the thought of this new life I am bringing forth into an unsafe place.

Sometimes Chris paints with me and sometimes he wanders.

I've been reading Leo's diary; another life laid down on paper. He had some beautiful ways to describe the village. His words add to the painting, carrying the weight of emotion about the place. It is April now and the days start off cool but bright, and the daffodils have been and gone. I found his entry from around this time and I'm layering it on top of what I can see from the window. It is a view ripe with memory, somehow.

The urn which contains my mother's ashes has been sitting on the mantelpiece since I moved back. I had a habit of talking to Ma for a little while; it was nice to feel she was with me as I made her house a home for me again.

Today though, I can't take my gaze from the jar, and it feels like the right day to let go. I reach up and take it down from the shelf. I cradle it close to me as I carry it up the main street of the village. It makes no sense, but I know what to do. I take the short cut down the road that runs by the Burns' farm, walk up the path and knock on the front door. It takes Vera a long time to answer. I imagine she has been upstairs, peering through the window to see who it is. Maybe she doesn't get many visitors. When she opens the door, I notice how small she seems in the doorway. She stares rigidly at me.

'Vera,' I begin. 'Can I come in?'

I half expect her to close the door in my face. I haven't spoken to her since the funeral. She says nothing but moves to one side, taking me into the sitting room and gesturing for me to sit while she stands in the doorway.

'Will you have a cup of tea?' she asks.

I nod reluctantly, thinking that this ritual is just prolonging the awkwardness.

She disappears back into the kitchen.

I look around the room, wondering who this woman really is. The fireplace is tiled in beige bricks. On its mantelpiece is a picture of her and George on their wedding day, their hands clasped tightly. I wonder how he spoke to her, what types of things he would say, whether she loved him. The lounge is feminine, framed pictures of flowers on the walls. It surprises me. Part of me wonders if she enjoys being without him. She reappears with a single cup of tea. I take a deep breath.

'I'm sorry about the funeral,' I say. I look down at my hands. 'My mother was sad when I was growing up,' I begin, 'that's what I remember the most about her, and I'm angry about that. That's what came out at the funeral, and I'm sorry that I took it out on you. You didn't deserve it.'

'I carry my family's problems,' she says, looking at me matter-of-factly.

'But that's just it; it wasn't George. It was Leo. I know that now.'

'But Leo was a Sedgwick; always wondered if he came back to pay us back somehow for what happened to his brother – the house that burned down.'

'But that was an accident too, wasn't it?' I say.

'What would you know about it? It was before your time.'

'I've heard the stories; a lamp left on,' I stutter, flustered.

'Our boy Eddie ran off afterwards,' she says, looking over my shoulder and out of the window. 'It was too much for him. He ran off and we never heard a word.'

I shake my head.

'And then one day, he wrote to me. Told me he was safe and that he had a good job. But that he could never come home.

'He left a return address, said not to show George, and I wrote back to tell him that his father passed eight years ago. It was fear that made him run and it was fear that kept him away.

'So, you see, it started with me, with my family. You've a right to be angry. What goes around comes around.'

'Vera,' I say, interrupting, 'the reason I've come today is to ask if I can sprinkle my mother's ashes on the farm. I felt like I should, to make peace or something. I don't know, I just felt like I wanted to. It's a strange idea, I suppose,' I say, backtracking, doubting myself.

Behind her glasses, I see tears forming. She nods.

'Shall we go right now?'

I finish my tea and Vera tidies away the things and goes out to the hallway to get her coat. She takes a red silk scarf and ties it around her head, the way my mother used to.

It's windy outside, but the sun is still bright. We walk

along to the big field, the one furthest from the house, and the wind pummels our stomachs, making us hunch over as we go. I steady Vera as we cross the field.

'I hope you'll enjoy being with Dad again, Ma,' I say into the wind.

I unscrew the lid of the urn and push it into my pocket to keep it from blowing away. I tip the urn to the side and watch as the grey flecks are snatched by the wind and race up into the sky.

I let her go, imagining she never comes down.

'Fly, Ma', I whisper, 'go and find Dad again.'

28

ALICE

July 2006

ESME ARRIVES one Monday morning in July. I feel a pain in the early hours, and I telephone the midwife at 5 am.

'Is there no one to help you?' she asks when I open the door for her.

I shake my head, and she helps me back up to the bedroom. Chris is out wandering, and I don't have the energy to worry about him.

And then later, amid the shouting and confusion and blood, this miracle of breath and bone appears.

Esme. Beloved.

She is a part of me in this world, but something so apart from me, so alone in herself. I am flooded with a love that I never knew existed.

When Christopher comes back, it is nearly lunchtime.

The midwife is packing up, and I am sitting up in bed, holding Esme.

I hear his heavy footsteps on the stairs, and he stands at the doorway.

'Alice, you alright? What have you got there? Oh! You had a baby!' he says, with astonishment, as if he'd forgotten she was coming. 'Oh, Alice, how did you do that so quickly?'

'Would you like to meet her?'

He nods and sits down at the end of the bed.

'This is Esme,' I say, putting her into his arms.

He is taken aback by her.

'Oh, Alice. She's so tiny. We'll have to take good care of her, won't we?'

'We will,' I nod. 'Chris, have we got anyone bringing us food today? I'm starving.'

'There's a cottage pie sitting on the doorstep and it's still warm. Shall I bring some up to you?'

'Yes please, Christopher.'

The midwife looks at me, concerned. She knows the situation and has been worried about it since the start.

I ring Sophie later and she agrees to come up on Wednesday to help.

That night, I decide to make some changes. I can't sleep with Chris wandering around outside, so I lock the back door and hide the key. I lock my bedroom door too, so that me and Esme are safe. Chris is such a nocturnal animal, and I don't feel like I can fully trust him anymore, not now. I don't want to leave myself open anymore; too much is at stake. But how can I look after them both at once, an over-grown child and a brand new one?

I hadn't foreseen it; I thought I'd just get here and see what would happen. I suppose I didn't believe Esme would be real until I held her in my arms.

But now she's here and everything is forever different.

29

———

CHRISTOPHER

J uly 2006

FUNNY NOW THAT Alice has had a baby. This wrinkled thing, like a piglet, all writhing and bony. I've got to be grown up, she says, I've not got to worry about things like animals and wandering.

She locks me in now, at night. Keeps me safe. But it makes me boil because I know I need the dark streets to soothe me. Mum told me I was different; I need to walk when I'm figuring things out, when I'm searching. So, I just tiptoe down the stairs, quiet as a mouse, and slide open the sash window, sneaking out like a robber into the silky night, where the darkness wraps around me. Leo lived outside and maybe I was born for it as well. She didn't think about the window, did she?

She don't have as much time for me as she used to; now it's all Esme this and Esme that. I hold her sometimes, when

Alice lets me, and I can see she's dreaming. Her little fingers prick up and she tries to clutch onto someone. She knows she's safe if someone holds her. Not too tight though, because I could crush her like a chicken if I tried. Alice said I must be as gentle as if she were a feather or a tiny mouse.

When she cries, her body judders and it goes right through her. She pulls up her knees and pinches up her eyes.

A new thing on my mind now. Es. I fetch her things from my walks. Yesterday, I stroked her face with a piece of corn. I thought she'd like it, the feeling on her cheek, but Alice saw me and leapt over to the crib.

'Christopher,' she said, 'you mustn't put things in there with her.'

'But she might like it, Alice. Showing her the world, that's all.'

'She doesn't need to see it yet, Christopher, save it for when she's bigger.'

She worries too much, Alice does. But I'll help where I can. She gets awful cross with me sometimes. Like today, I fetched this mouse in from the field and showed it to Esme up close, like. She flailed her arms around and hit it away from my hand, so it fell into the crib and started scuttling around in her hair.

Alice came running in.

'Christopher, what are you doing?' she shouted, and Esme started crying even louder.

'A mouse! What the hell are you putting a mouse in her crib for?'

And then I looked at her and she was rocking Esme too fast, joggling her around and crying herself.

I scooped it up and put it out of the window. And then I stood there with my hands over my ears, looking at the lines of the furrows running straight to the horizon. When Alice shouts, it all gets too much. My hands hold out the world. I can't bear the weight of her rage pointed at me. The thing is I get so many things wrong.

'Sorry, Alice,' I said. 'I'm sorry.'

'Christopher!'

She turned me around, Esme still up on her chest and pulled one hand away from my ear. She looked me straight in the face.

'Babies need to be clean. Do you understand? You can't show anything from the garden to Esme, not yet, certainly not things that are alive. And you need to wash your hands. Before you touch her again, you always need to make sure you have washed your hands. Do you understand?'

I nod, my face burning, my heart racing.

30

———

ALICE

July 2006

Soph comes up and cries when she sees Es again. Sits with us, makes tea, washes up and is generally an angel for 48 hours.

I take her up to the studio and show her what I've been working on.

'These are good Al,' she says. 'Really good.'

'Do you think? It's just the more I look, the more I see. I'm trying to unpack that, I guess. And all the layers of memory in this place.'

'It's sucked you right in hasn't it, this village?'

'Yeah, it has,' I say, laughing.

I hug her goodbye at the train station and she says, 'Do you want me to tell Pete about Es?'

I feel scared suddenly. After all, she is half his. I suddenly wish he didn't know anything about her.

'He said he didn't want to know, didn't he? His choice.'

'Ok, sure. Well, let me know if you change your mind. I love you.'

She kisses me on the cheek and runs for her train.

THE HOUSE FEELS empty after she is gone.

Chris and I try to be family in the only way we know how; we paint, we walk, we watch TV. I am dog-tired; a carer for him and her.

I DON'T HEAR from Sophie for months. Then, in September, a call.

'Al, how's it going?' she says, her voice so bright and quick.

'Soph! It's been ages!'

'I know, things have been mental. So, you know we applied for funding to develop the art space?'

'Yeah,' I reply.

'Well, we only went and got a hundred grand!'

'Bloody Hell!'

'I know, it's mad. It means we can extend into the next-door unit, and we can afford to put on exhibitions. We'd love your latest collection to be our inaugural show.'

'Oh, wow,' I say.

Here I am, out in the wilds in more ways than one, hope-less at networking, and she offers my biggest dream to me on a plate.

'Mate, look, I don't want any favours,' I say, sitting there in bed with Esme.

She is four months old. It has been a whirlwind of

cuddles and washing and Christopher. Keeping him happy, keeping him away.

'Fuck's sake, it's not a favour. Your work is really good.'

'What about Es?'

'What about Es? She'll come too. Stop making barriers for yourself.'

'But Soph, I get no time at all to myself. None but the dead of night, where I lock myself and Esme away. It's not fair on Christopher, I know, but I don't know how else to protect myself. And I like being around him in the day; it's just the nights, just when I am asleep and I can't look after her.'

'Al, you've taken on too much. I can come up a couple of weekends so you've got time to finish the collection.'

'Would you do that?'

'Course I would ... I've shown Nick the ropes at the cafe, so I can get away a little bit more. Anyway, it won't be ready until December. But we can have a show, fairy lights, a jazz pianist, your paintings on the walls. I can't wait, Al.'

'Shit. Neither can I.'

31

ALICE

September 2006

WE GO BACK to the mouth of the Nene often, looking out to the Wash and the sky. It is harder now with Esme; we have to time it so that she falls asleep in the car. I bundle her up in the pushchair, covered in blankets, and we paint until she wakes. We both need it.

Today, Christopher has made great sweeps of grey and blue across his canvas, the birds a scrape of black. He stands there for hours sometimes, trying to distil the essence of that sky. What a pair we make, both of us needing this language of colour, of mood. For me, it tells me who I am; for him, it helps him to remember. And remembering is sometimes what we need.

'There's something I need to do,' he says, 'that might help me to get better. Will you let me paint her?'

'Who?' I ask.

'You know who.'

For, of course, there is something else that he knows like the back of his hand, that he has seen a thousand times in his mind's eye: Cassie. He paints her portrait, just as she was on the last day with her yellow Alice band and her pigtails. She is smiling in the painting, and I am glad for it.

I've read Leo's words so many times now, that the journal is falling apart in my hands. I think of him and his words when I look out to sea, and think of the Fens, this whole land, pulled from water. Coming out here makes me feel smaller, which I am glad for. It helps me to put things into perspective.

AND THAT IS why we are tied down, hemmed into these small lives, under this big sky. We used to be islands, see, each one to himself, bit like these marshlands, tufts of land, unconnected, like. Then they drained the land and saw we were all one. Each little thing affects another, little by little. So, you see, there's no such thing as a wanderer really, no such thing as islands no more.

LEO CAME to the village wanting to stay a loner, detached from the place, but it got its roots into him, got right into his heart.

That's why he loved Ma, because love is in our nature.

32

ALICE

September 2006

I THINK BACK to the first painting I did on that first day in Ma's house. I dated it: 3.6.05. You would think it was boring, but to me there was everything in that view, all the details of a life unhindered. The trees blowing in the wind, a sense of freedom.

I feel a kinship with Leo, the more I read of his diary:

THERE MIGHT BE A COIN, glinting in the soil, the rustle of a small creature moving away, a caterpillar with his nose in the air, deciding which way to go next. In the field, the wallpaper is the sky. It comes right down to the ground, full of colour and mood all day long. There's the clear sun up with the tufts of puffy cloud floating by and the look of the sun creeping down at the end of the day, its red wings settling over the land, spreading its glow over the furrows. Then there are other days, when the clouds are drawn across the sky like fine white scars. It seems that everything would come from that sky, the news of the weather, the end of the world, the sadnesses that fall like rain.

FUNNY how that's what I look out on, but what I am living is so different. I don't have to worry about money, for one. I don't have a mortgage to worry about, so it is just bills and food. When Christopher moved in, I started receiving Carer's Allowance, and that helps. Christopher gets money too, so Ben has arranged a standing order to my account for food. Christopher didn't bother with his bank, he never wanted anything. There will be Ma's inheritance, too. I got a letter last week, saying she had £30,000 saved up. It said it would be paid into my account within the month. Funny to get a windfall – you always think it'll change your life, but your life is your life, isn't it? It's what you do each day. It's nice to know the money is there but it won't change anything.

OVER THE NEXT FEW MONTHS, we gear up slowly to the exhibition. It feels so good to have my friends, these canvases, around me. I feel so full up of the Fens, like I have imbibed its ways over the last year and a half. I have taken in Leo, Ma's house, Christopher. I have felt the house make its way through the seasons, and I have painted my way through with it. Through the grief over Ma, the emptiness after Pete, the promise of Esme and the confusion of Christopher. I prop the canvases up in the dining room and feel the changing of the year all around me. They show the warmth of autumn, the low sun and later mornings, the battle of winter, the hard ground and pale sun, flamboyant spring, dangerous summer; all the signs of a life well loved.

The exhibition is the first time that Christopher has been away with me. I think it might be the first time he's ever left the village. I ask him but he says he can't remember. We pack carefully, bringing things that remind him of home, his book about Cassie and his sketchbook.

We drive down to Cambridge on the first Saturday in December and are there by lunchtime.

Soph pulls open the door and pulls me into a hug.

How disorienting it is to be back here but with Christopher. In some ways it feels like I have never left; in some ways everything is new. Esme is five months now. Sophie and Nick are amazing with her.

I am not jealous like I thought I would be of Soph and Nick, of their freedom. I don't think my work has ever looked so good. I am on a journey that I never would have been on had I stayed in Cambridge.

We bring some of Christopher's work too, just to show it to the guys, and they are amazed at his language and his use of the oils.

'We've got to put these up,' Sophie says. 'Christopher, these are wonderful.'

He smiles.

Sophie touches him on the arm.

'I'm not just saying that Christopher, they really are wonderful.'

'Thank you,' he says, bashfully.

We hang our pieces for the opening night and later, there we are, in a city, in a room strung with lightbulbs, and yet full of windows opening out onto fields. There are skies on each side of the room, lifting the lid off this place. How has it come to this? I think, and I feel like I could burst with pride.

I carry Esme in the sling, and she sleeps next to my heart.

'Is Pete coming?' I whisper to Soph.

She takes my hand. 'We haven't told him about it, but it's an open exhibition so if he walks in, we can't really stop him.'

I nod and take a deep breath. I can handle this.

I squeeze Chris' hand and say, 'Are you proud? Can you believe we're doing this? All my life I've waited for an exhibition and here you are gate-crashing it! You deserve it though, Christopher. I think you've found your language.'

He smiles and puts his arm around me, and I feel peace for once. I hold it and long to keep it. I beam like a crazed thing and cry tipsy tears.

Sophie steps up to the microphone and introduces me, and I walk up to the front of a room full of people with Esme still sleeping on my chest, and it feels like a parallel universe. I have been living another life for the last two years, one away from people, from noise, from shops. We've been living in our own little world.

I begin slowly.

'Thanks so much for coming, everyone. The collection is called *Under a Fenland Sky*. It is a portrait seen through the skies of the village where I live. Many people don't leave the village; they stay for a lifetime. And it seems that there is nothing and yet everything there. I left a long time ago and came here, to Cambridge. I was desperate for people, for anonymity, for the city, but then something drew me back to it, and I returned, and it feels like a faithful friend now.

'We seem a strange tribe, the villagers. We understand and revere the sky and the land, for all they give and all they can snatch away in an instant. I paint the sky outside my window, and each day it is a miracle, each day it is new.

'There's a journal that I found, written by a friend of mine who died a long time ago. He lived outside, he was at one with the world. He knew his place in it. I've taken his words and used them to help me portray the feel of the place. So, while this is a portrait of the village, it is also a portrait of Leo, our lovely friend, and all of the words that he couldn't speak in his lifetime.

'I'm exhibiting tonight with my friend Christopher, who paints too. His paintings tell their own story; he sees things in the sky that I cannot.

'Do you want to say something, Chris?' I ask, looking over to him and then instantly regretting it.

He looks as if he might, but then shakes his head.

As I am talking, I notice a man who looks like he is in his sixties. He watches me intently as I talk and looks as if he wants to interrupt me to say something.

'We hope you enjoy the work, and thanks again for coming.'

After I finish speaking, he comes straight up to me, and he looks for a moment like a long-lost friend.

'Which village are you from?' he asks me, and I tell him.

'I'm Edmund,' he says. 'I used to live there too.'

'You're Vera's boy,' I gasp. 'She told me about you.'

He nods, and almost flinches, as if he's scared of what she's said about him.

'This is Christopher,' I say.

There is a flash of recognition in his eyes. He takes a breath.

'You were the boy,' he says, 'with Cassie. I was the man on the bus. I tried to help.'

I panic at the thought of Chris's reaction in a place far

from home. He waits for a moment, then says, 'There weren't nothing you could do. You tried.'

Christopher reaches out to touch him on the arm.

'It ain't your fault she died. She just did.'

He surprises me with how calm and measured he is.

'I've never forgotten her,' Edmund says.

'Nor have I,' Christopher says.

And she hangs between us then, this ghost of Cassie, the girl that never grew up, that never left the village, and my heart sinks as I realise that she ties us together and we will never be free from her.

But it astounds me too, that in a place far from home, a loose end can be tied up, and a connection can be made. It makes me wonder if life starts as a muddle, but as we grow, we tie up all the loose ends, or whether it starts out neat and we make it worse as we go on.

Now that we are in a new place, the thought strikes me that perhaps it is the village that keeps Christopher captive. Every corner he turns reminds him of Cassie. What if we were to leave, I wonder? Would we be able to start afresh? Would she fade in his memory like an old story? Could we make a new life somewhere else?

33

THE VILLAGE

December 2006

WHAT THEY DON'T KNOW as they stand there talking to Edmund about the girl is that their lives are entwined in more ways than one.

For he was the boy that caused the burning. Alice knew he was running, but from what his mother didn't say. It wasn't Edmund's father that caused the fire as Leo had thought. It was Edmund who set the cottage alight and made Leo's brother homeless. And he was only a boy, a boy desperate to escape his father's rage. He did the only thing he could think of to get him out of the place. And it was Leo who arrived one day to avenge his brothers' eviction, and it was him who laid the poisoned trap that squeezed all the love and life right out of Alice's father. We saw from above how they were all bound to each other, with these invisible strings of malice, loyalty, love, rage.

That whole village is tied in knots, same as other villages, to be sure, but we stick to our own, there are too many voices, else.

What Christopher and Alice couldn't see was Edmund's thoughts, reeling, as the exhibition took him right back to the village, to the place he'd been trying for so long to leave. He had rehearsed the story over and over so many times, but he had never spoken it aloud. He had never been back. For in the end, the price of his sanity was his family. He chose a peaceful life where he could walk out in quiet mornings, without guilt. But what about his mother? His brother? We heard their thoughts, the ones who managed to leave and the ones left behind; the ones who spent their days watching at the windows, longing for something to change.

And although he'd never spoken it aloud, he'd written it down, in a letter to his mother. He had put his address on the first letter, an act of great courage because he didn't know if his father was still living. But when his mother wrote back to tell him that he had passed, he wrote to her again with his confession. Of course, his mother could guess it all anyway, for why else would he disappear? And we had watched over him as he wrote and rewrote the damn thing, as he picked up each word and pressed it into his heart. He knew it so well; he lived and breathed his confession, but he'd never found the courage to put on the stamp and to put it in the postbox, because he couldn't bear to lose her love.

MOTHER.

One day I did stand up to Father and a house went up in flames, in acres of farmland, in the middle of harvest. I had to do it; I couldn't see any other way. I would even say I delighted in the roar of the flames, letting out a whoop as they swallowed the house. There was a second where it went from being just partly alight, the flame a numb little thing, to being completely engulfed. Then the house was drowning in red and orange. My whole ribcage was shaking as I watched it burn, not believing it was my small hands that had done it.

I imagined it was Father, his skin and bone that were burning. If it got me out of there, then I'd have been glad. If it got me to prison, I'd have been glad. Four close walls instead of the endless ditches and fields of the Fens any day.

Poor Jonathan, though, I laid the blame on him and gave myself a reason to burn it down. Said he'd been dossing about on the farm, and it made Father's anger boil over.

Later that night, the guilt began to rot in my gut. I couldn't stop thinking about Jonathan, who'd only ever worked hard and been honest and kind to me. His father, Edward, worked on the farm too and things had been strained between him and Father already. I'd only said it were him to cover myself, but I couldn't bear to see what Father would do to him the next day. I was trying to sleep but my eyes kept popping open. I remember mouthing the words to myself. 'What can I do?' I said. 'How can I stop it?' I knew that I shouldn't let him get punished for what I did. It weren't fair.

When the idea first came, I pushed it down. But then it wouldn't go away. It would have to be quick if I were to do it at all. And I knew I had to. I reasoned that if the Sedgwicks weren't working the land anymore, if they didn't live there, then Father couldn't get to them, especially not Jonathan. This voice kept coming into my head saying that I had to. It was the only way out.

It was that same night that I did it. It had to be.

I got that thing in my gut like butterflies flitting about. It wouldn't go away or be still.

I waited til they were all out and poured the petrol in a crack where a window had been left ajar. It made a slapping sound when it hit the floorboards inside and I shut my eyes as I carried on pouring. I took a deep breath as I struck the match and dropped it in. It terrified me how easy it was. It made a sound, a whoomph, when the flame caught, and I felt for once that I had a sort of power. I felt cut free.

I had done it, something brave. Something he'd have been proud of me for.

Everyone thought I was in my bedroom reading. I ran across the field and climbed back in with no one hearing a sound. I sat on my bed and tried to read, tried to still my heartbeat, tried to breathe normally.

If no one knew it were me, it couldn't have been, could it? If my heart stilled and they couldn't smell the petrol, then I had got away with it.

It was a shout that I heard first and then James burst in saying, 'Have you seen the flames? The Sedgwick house is burning.'

I tried to look as if I didn't know a thing about it. It wasn't hard. I hadn't done that, had I? That wall of flames? It couldn't have been me.

And then a little part of me thought I had gone too far. But the idea had run away with me. And it was so absurd, it was so far away from me that it couldn't have been me. Already, I had almost convinced myself.

One of the last times I saw father, he was dozing in front of the fire, his pipe hanging from his mouth. I came into the room after dinner to do some reading and then heard his snores. I stood there listening for a while and went upstairs to read.

It had an air of finality about it, when I think back to it, that scene, with me standing in the corner, just listening.

I knew then I had to make myself disappear.

HE RAN, dear boy, because he didn't know how to make right what he had done. And we loved him all the while that he ran. But didn't he know it would be easier to stand up to his father? Didn't he know that that would be better than robbing his own family blind?

34

—————

ALICE

December 2006

THE NEXT MORNING, Sophie takes us walking around Cambridge. We walk over to the Christmas market on Parker's Piece, searching for that elusive Christmassy feeling. This year, for the first time, I have my own little heart, my own little someone to love and cherish. It will be a strange one, with Christopher, but we are family, and we will settle down into it like we always do. A turkey from the butcher, all the trimmings, Ben and the family over at some point, perhaps. But all that can wait. The sweet smell of a street vendor's churros is already wafting around the morning city air. I miss this place, I think. But then I remember how different my life is now: a baby, an exhibition, Christopher. Three things that do not seem to go together.

The market is already bustling, and we walk around the stalls, looking at the wooden crafts and various delicacies on offer. We turn the corner and Christopher bumps into a man carrying two coffees.

Shit. I know that face. Pete. But we've all seen each other now so we can't pretend we haven't. He looks tired and hassled. He is wearing a stripy top and a beanie.

'Pete! Hi!' I say, pretending to be pleased to see him.

'Hi!' he says, scanning the faces.

'This is Christopher,' I say, making no mention of the baby in the sling.

He looks at him, with a puzzled expression, then at me, then at the sling.

'And this is?'

I feel vulnerable, exposed, naked, and don't want to show her face but before I can stop myself, I am saying, 'This is Esme.'

Esme, heart of my heart. Protected one.

I hate to say it, but I watch his face crumble. She is his own flesh and blood, what would anyone else do? What does it feel like to see your DNA made beautiful? Had he thought of us at all? Did he know I'd even had her?

But he asks no more questions and makes his excuses to get away.

He had told me, hadn't he, in the restaurant that night that he wanted nothing to do with me, nothing to do with her? But she is real now and before she was just a figment of our imagination. It is different.

Soph ushers me and Christopher away and I laugh it off, but my armpits have begun to prickle with sweat. I wish I hadn't shown him her face, wish I hadn't told her his name. Wish we hadn't bumped into him at all.

I quiz Sophie on him later, before we leave.

'So, do you see him much these days?'

'We bump into him sometimes. Nick doesn't really see him – he's sold out, got an office job.'

'Did you tell him about Esme?'

'No. You asked me not to.'

'So, he didn't know he had a daughter until today?'

She shrugs. 'Look, he knew you were pregnant. He could have called. Do not in your goodness think that you owe him anything. You don't owe him anything.'

I nod. I'm exhausted. I need to get home.

Later, we bundle all of our possessions into the car and head back along the A10 to the village. The windows are steamed up and I feel sick. The rain streams down the panes and feels like all the tears I want to cry. And it's not because I miss him, not because I want to be with him, but because life just seems so broken sometimes, and there is no way of fixing it, no way at all.

35

ALICE

October 2006

CHRIS SURPRISES ME. He is good with Esme, these days. In some ways, it isn't as hard as I thought it would be. He takes his meds, he goes to therapy, we walk a lot. He paints.

Esme makes him laugh; she brings a purpose and a lightness to our days.

'Chris, have you ever thought about leaving the village?' I ask him again one day, a few months after the exhibition.

'Why would we want to do that?'

'I just wondered if it might help you to, you know, forget.'

'But I don't want to forget.'

'But it might be easier to get on with things, to move forward. We could move to Cambridge, or another city. Would you like that?'

He frowns and thinks for a while.

'But what would we paint, Alice?'

'I hadn't thought of that. It's just an idea,' I shrug.

He looks at Esme, who is sitting up on her own, chewing a toy giraffe.

'What will she want with a city? She'll be just like Cassie when she's bigger, you'll see. We'll go running across the fields, it'll be just like old times.'

'No, Chris, she won't be anything like Cassie. She's her own person.'

I wonder if the older she gets, the more she will become her to him, and then I push the thought away.

THE VILLAGE

And slowly, the years trickle by, like an underground stream.

Pete doesn't call.

Chris, Alice and Esme put down their roots, and they find they are unable to pull them up again.

Even if she wants to. Even if he wants to.

Why don't Alice and Esme leave? Go and find somewhere new? Who can say?

Perhaps they have forgotten how to change things, perhaps they are the type of people who don't change something unless it breaks. But when the person is yourself, why wait so long? Why not be kinder to yourself?

We watch them and long for happiness, however complicated a thing that is.

We wish for joy, pure and simple, for this the oddest of couples, joined at the heart, tethered at the ankles.

37

CHRISTOPHER

M ay 2013

WHEN I SLEEP I can see her there in my mind and then I wake and all the spiders crawl down over my eyes and I know that if I could just find her I could bring her home I can feel it in my legs my heart I lost her didn't I Mum? I know it was my fault I remember her mother crumpling at the roadside all of her loss pouring out onto the street just like blood broad daylight and I stood there needing a pee wondering how to turn back time even a few minutes you see the thing with fault is that it could be anyone's really no one would know unless they were there would they no one knew no one would know no need to panic no need to press charges on any of it no one would know unless I told them Leo Cass and me that's all and no one heard except me and her I know that she'll come back with me when I find her and then I can make it all right again there must be a way to make it right again I'm just so worried that she's angry with me I would be if I was robbed of this all what is life for with all its sweetness and birdsong what is it for if we can't make things right again turn the clock backwards? Sometimes I hear her voice deep down in my ribcage so small and I know that she's hiding in there folded within me inside of me I know that sounds wrong but it's true I know it you might think I'm crazy but I'm not crazy and if I try so so hard and scrunch my eyes and my fists to tiny balls then I can hear her I have to concentrate so so hard but when I do I can hear what she's saying. 'Cassie,' I whisper into myself, to her, 'Cassie, come back, I can't live without you.'

38

ALICE

Mʏ 2013

Wᴇ ᴀʀᴇ ᴅɪɢɢɪɴɢ up some of the spring carrots that we planted, all bundled up in our coats. Esme's cheeks are bright pink, and her eyes shine in the dusk glow. It is Friday and we have the best of things: a full weekend that stretches away from us.

I go inside to boil the kettle for tea. When I come out again, there are two trowels laid on the ground and no sign of Chris and Esme.

I shout after her, 'Esme!', as loud as I can. She must be within earshot; she must be. Unless they ran. And then it strikes me that he must have timed it. Just as I went inside, he must have scooped her up and ran. A sickly feeling rises in my stomach.

I squeeze through a hole in the hedgerow into the horse field, and I can see two figures up at the far end. He looks as if he is trying to put her over the fence onto the back of some fallow fields.

'Thank fuck for that,' I say under my breath, before shouting, 'Chris! Esme!'

And they turn. Frozen.

I run as fast as I can to the top of the field and, when I get there, bend over to catch my breath, panting, my hands on my knees.

He stops what he is doing. Stands and looks straight at me.

'What are you doing?' I say, between breaths.

'Just showing her the fields,' he says, all nonchalant.

'Chris! You can't do this,' I say, between breaths.

'Mummy,' Esme says and comes to me. She puts her hand to my ear and moves my hair out of the way before whispering, 'He showed me a dead bird, Mummy, his head all smashed in.'

'Fuck's sake Chris, why are you showing her roadkill? She's only six.'

'Me and Cassie went off, like, when we were young,' he says, as if it's a justification. 'I ain't harming her.'

'I don't care. You're not taking my daughter. Where were you going anyway?'

'Oh, just somewhere.'

I stare at him.

'You can't take her out on your own, Chris. She's not old enough. If you want to go out walking, I come too. Do you understand?'

He nods and kicks at some sticks on the ground, but I know it's not sinking in.

'You timed it, didn't you? You ran as soon as I went inside,' I say, and I scare myself with the implication, realising I have made it all the more real by saying it out loud.

He doesn't answer but looks down and scuffs the dirt with his shoe. He knows that I know.

'Come on, Es,' I say, curling my arm protectively around her shoulder.

I have grown cold towards Chris over the years. Since the moment Esme came into the world, he has been second best. It couldn't be any other way; Es is my flesh and blood and I will protect her with everything that I am. Chris can't see that, though. He doesn't understand why I can't trust him.

He was once the central axis to my day but, now, has become a comet hurtling through the sky, headed for destruction. It feels like a battle is raging, within these four small walls, and that soon, something will break. I'm damned if I let it be her.

I could ring Ben. The thought is always there. But the thought of his condescending tone, the thought of them knowing that our lives are screwed up, that I can't cope, makes me rage inside. It's not so bad, I always think. It's not so bad. And so I wait a little longer.

But sometimes it is so bad, and I'm not sure it will ever change.

I GET HOME and lock the door. Es wants to watch a cartoon, so I set her up in her favourite armchair and go through to the kitchen. I ring Soph. I feel like I have been backed into a corner and I don't know what to do.

She answers straight away, though I can tell she's at the cafe.

'Hi Al!'

'Hi. Chris just tried to walk off with Es. I don't know

what to do,' I say, my chest still pounding. I pace up and down in the tiny kitchen.

'Ok. What was he trying to do with her?'

'They were just walking. I don't know. I don't know if it was innocent or if there's more to it. I've got a really bad feeling that we're heading to a car crash, and I don't know how I can stop it.'

'Can you speak to Ben? Get a psych review? Want to come and stay for a bit?'

'I don't know if I can.'

There is quiet on the line for a few moments, and then she adds, 'Hon, if they were just going for a walk, then it sounds like you've got nothing to worry about.'

I sigh.

'Yes, but it's not that. There's something else. He planned it. He waited until I went inside and then they ran.'

'He'd never hurt her.'

'I know.'

I wanted to test the theory by saying it out loud. And it worked. It's ridiculous and Soph thinks so too. He would never hurt her.

I hear the hiss of the coffee machine behind her. I just want to be with her, for her to wrap her arms around me. I want to escape to her flat, where the walls are pink, and everything feels safe. I wipe away a tear and take a deep breath.

'Love you, Soph. Got to go.'

I hang up feeling calmer just for having said the words out loud, for having verbalised my worst fears. It makes me realise that I need to make a change though. Even if it's ridiculous, even if I'm paranoid. I call Ben.

'Hey, I need you to come over. Chris just tried to walk off with Es, I don't think she's safe here.'

'I'll come in a few weeks,' he says. 'We're going to France on Monday.'

'A few weeks? I need you here now. I can't do it anymore, Ben,' I say. 'I can't. He needs to come to yours or go to an institution. I know it's cruel, but more and more, I just don't feel safe here. I don't feel Es is safe with him. He's a good guy, I know he is, but I just don't trust him anymore.'

'Do you think it's his medication? Have you been in touch with Dr Skinner?'

'No. It could be. It could be a thousand things. But I think it's Es. I think it's because she's nearly seven.'

He pauses. Realising that that's how old Cassie was.

'Look. I'll sort something out. I'll talk to Anna. Maybe there's a residential place near us. Maybe there's one here. We'll change something. Just hold tight.'

I want to grab him by the head and shake it. I don't think he sees the urgency. I'm worried that two weeks will be too late.

39

———

THE VILLAGE

J une 2013

HIS MOTHER always said to him that he would never leave, that he was a faithful dog yapping at her heels, that she didn't know where he'd go if it wasn't to her back door. His father always said he didn't need to leave the Fens, that there was nothing outside for him and why should there be for Chris either? Ben left them all so easily and it felt like a betrayal.

But Christopher is stuck now, stuck in the mud, with voices swirling around him and the one hard voice within him.

When so many people tell him what he should do, how can he know who to believe? The voices push in on him, like the dark blue-grey waves of the sea; tilting up on the horizon, bending the truth around him and sometimes he can't stand with the weight of it, and he doesn't know what is true anymore. So many people telling him what to think, what to do, how to move on.

Us long gone ones know that Cassie is still everything for him. The girl with sunshine in her hair. Just one thought of her takes him back to a time when nothing was broken. And what can we say, as wise as we are? We don't know what it is like to lose someone, for we never have. We gather them to ourselves instead.

His only consolations now are the cold sweep of a breeze when he looks into a wintry sunset and the pang of joy when he wakes to the sound of birdsong. Healing is under our skin, all around us, and we hope with our knotty bones that he will find his. He must find it for himself, you see. That is the way of these things. There is only so much we can do.

Christopher leans on the fence, looking out at the horses in the paddock and watching the sky fall to a smudgy pink. He stands up straight and we see him resolve in his heart to fight his way out past the stormy waters of his family's voices, to go after her and to find her again. Cassie is the only thing he is moving onwards for. He isn't giving up.

And all our hearts break as we watch him make the wrong choice again.

40

ALICE

J uly 2013

I SEE him looking at Esme sometimes and I know what he is thinking. She wears her hair in pigtails, too. She is coming up for seven in two weeks, but I will her to grow quicker, to get through this phase and become herself again at the other end of it.

Christopher is lost in the dream of her, of who he wants her to be. He often calls her Cassie instead of Esme.

One Saturday, she says, 'Mum, please can Chris take me for a walk?'

'Erm, not just yet sweetie. Why don't you wait until after lunch and we can all go together?'

'I don't want you to come! Chris said he's got something to show me.'

'Honey,' I say, taking her upstairs, and saying in an urgent whisper, 'we've talked about Chris before. He doesn't understand things like you and I do and you've got to be careful. He doesn't know how to keep you safe.'

She sighs but I think she understands on some level. I watch her go back out to the garden where she plays hide and seek with Chris. I stand in the doorway, listening.

'You're nearly seven now, ain't you?' Chris says.

Esme nods.

'Just like Cassie when she ran away.'

'What happened to her, Chris?'

'No one really knows what happened to her, she just vanished one day and didn't come to say goodbye.'

I don't correct him. How can I tell my daughter that his friend was killed in our village at the same age as her?

'It's your turn to count, Chris!' Esme shouts, and she runs around to the front of the house.

He follows her, and I can hear him as he circles around to the front of the house. She is there in the corner of the front lawn, hiding under a bush. I can see a flash of her pink joggers.

They have something special, I think, something innocent. A friendship. It is okay. I breathe deeply, trying to still my panicked heart.

He's harmless, I think. He's just simple. He doesn't understand things like I do. But still, my palms become clammy and my heart thumps. I cannot take my eyes off them.

She squeals as he finds her and shouts out, 'My turn!' as Chris runs off to hide. 'ONE, TWO, THREE, FOUR, FIVE, SIX, SEVEN, EIGHT, NINE, TEN. Ready or not here I come!'

I hear the beat of her footsteps on the concrete path, and she disappears behind the old chicken shed trying to find him.

I stand there with those two running about me, and I feel so tired. I am on guard, all the time. I can never switch off. I stand there wondering when this will all change, wondering how I can hold this ever-changing dynamic in my hands, wondering if, in the end, it will break me.

41

THE VILLAGE

August 2013

CHRISTOPHER WAKES. He goes downstairs to make himself breakfast and there is Esme, already sitting at the kitchen table with her brown hair tied into scruffy bunches.

'Good morning, little one,' he says.

'Hello, Christopher,' she says, 'what are you doing today?'

He sits down opposite her and thinks for a moment.

'I've got a painting to finish later, but we could go for a walk if you'd like.'

'Do you think Mummy will mind?'

'I shouldn't think so, I'll always look after you. We won't be long.'

They put on coats and shoes.

'Now, where does Alice put the key?' Christopher asks.

'I know! It's in here,' Esme says, opening a drawer and finding it in a mustard tin at the back. 'I've seen her.'

'Good girl.'

Christopher takes the key and unlocks the door, and they walk quietly down the path into the morning.

42

ALICE

 ugust 2013

I WAKE TO A QUIET HOUSE. My heart starts to thump as soon as I realise that Esme isn't in the room. I must have forgotten to lock the bedroom door. Maybe she crept downstairs first thing. Her shoes are gone. The back door is unlocked. How did Chris find the key?

'Shit,' I say.

I run out in my pyjamas and wellies.

'Chris? Esme?'

But I don't know where to start because I don't know how long they've been gone.

'Fuck, fuck, fuck,' I say under my breath. 'This can't be happening.'

The panic sets off immediately in me. I screwed up. I took my eye off the ball for a second. I slept. My fingers buzz and my heart races. My mind crashes with questions.

I run up the main road through the village and stop at the shop.

'Have you seen Chris and Esme?'

Lynn, the shopkeeper, shakes her head.

'No, sorry.'

'I need you to help me. My daughter has gone off with Chris. He's taken her.'

'Oh, he wouldn't hurt a fly, no need to panic.'

I slam both of my hands down on the desk, and say, 'You don't know what he'd do and neither do I.'

She swallows nervously. She has never liked me, not for a second since the moment I moved here, tearing up the village rules. But she knows I'm right. I stand there and call 999. I don't know what else to do.

'YOU'VE GOT to help me, please,' I say down the phone, the tears coming and the phone trembling in my hand. 'My daughter is seven. The man I live with, he's not stable, he's taken her. He might hurt her. I don't know what to do.'

'Okay,' says the call handler. 'Try not to panic. We will get someone out to you as soon as we can.'

'Please come now.'

I want to run but I don't know which direction to go in. All the possibilities spread out in front of me like a map. I run up to the farm, across the fields, around all the places I can think of. It is early. 8.30 am. They can't have got far. But I don't know when they left. I ask the early workers if they've seen anyone, and they shake their heads.

My heart races as I try to think clearly, but I can't because my brain is spinning out of control. Every heartbeat says, 'Where is she, where is she, where is she?'

I stop and call Ben, my fingers trembling as I find his name in my contacts list.

'He's taken her!' I shout as soon as he picks up, and my voice breaks.

'My God,' Ben says, softly.

'I knew he would. I told you he wasn't safe. I told you I needed help. I told you time was running out. Where is he? Where would he be?'

But I can't breathe, and I can't talk. Tears choke my voice.

Ben speaks slowly. I can hear him eating air, the shock pressing him to clay, stopping up his tongue.

'I, I ... did you try Mum's plot? The hedgerow? Leo's greenhouse?'

I've tried them all, I want to say, but I can't even get the words out. The tears seep out of my eyes, and I fall to the floor. My chest is heaving. I've been running since I woke.

'You have to fix this, Ben,' I croak.

'I'm coming now,' he says and hangs up.

43

ALICE

I CAN'T THINK, I can't eat, I can't breathe because you are not here. Esme, breath of mine, daughter of my heart, how could I let this happen to you? Night falls and I am walking all over, like he does. I am walking, calling your name, Esme, Esme, and then, in rage, Christopher. The sniffer dogs are out. Noses in ditches, their silky pelts running over the fields. Everyone around me blurs into a mass of cowering sympathy. 'They'll find her, love,' they say. 'He wouldn't hurt a fly,' but it is pitch black and the bats squeak in the trees, the owls hoot and still you have not come home. I will never sleep, never stop, never eat until I find you again. My legs are lead but I walk – I stumble – over ditches and fields. I scrape my arms on brambles, crawl along the backs of hedgerows, call your names over and over again until my voice is broken and sore.

'Rest,' the voices say, 'you must rest,' but how can I rest when my daughter isn't here? How can I sleep when she isn't with me?

Two days I don't sleep don't eat don't wash can't sit still can't be inside if you are not. I swear I could go insane.

I need you daughter my breath my only hope in a dark world.

I'll never forgive myself if he lays a finger on you.

ALICE

I CATCH my breath in the corner of a field. It is dusk, Saturday. Soph is here. She drove from Cambridge in the time that my daughter wasn't with me. Ben is here, too, now. It's been a whole night and two days. I am empty. I am insane. How could I have let this happen?

We are a few miles out from the village, calling endlessly, our voices hoarse.

I get a call from the policeman.

'The dogs are onto something,' he says. 'Come out to the junction by Land's Farm.'

I DRIVE THERE, my throat sore, my body exhausted. The sun has baked the field to a crust, I shield my eyes against the low sun to see. I stumble out of the car and there is a small crowd of people there already and she is there, and they are carrying her back towards me across the field, her small body in their arms.

'Es,' I say, pushing my way through the gathering of people at the field's edge. I strain my eyes to see her, to see if she's ok, to see if she's breathing, if she's moving.

A policeman carries her. Her arms are up around his neck, and she is leaning her head on him.

'Es!' I shout and I am running to her, as fast as I can, across the stubble.

And then they are in front of me, and they lower her down onto my lap and we sink onto the furrows. I hold her close to me and I can breathe again.

Her whole body trembles and she is as light as anything.

'Mum,' she whispers.

I bury my face into the crook of her neck.

I smell her fine hair and feel her warm skin pressed against my cheek.

He tried to take her from me.

Es.

He had her, he took her away from me, he ran with her.

My Es. Everything I have in this world.

For two whole days.

But now she is here in my arms, held tight in the circle of my love.

Here with me.

The relief washes over me like a flood and the sobs shake my whole core.

I hold her away from me for a moment and look her in the face. It is pale in the sunlight. She must have been so scared.

· · ·

THE PARAMEDICS CHECK ES OVER, wrap her in a blanket and do her obs. They give her a bottle of water and a ham sandwich, which she nibbles hungrily. They say they'll take her into the hospital overnight for monitoring, and I am relieved as we get into the ambulance and pull away. A white room, me and my baby girl. No chance of him finding us. I sob with relief all the way there.

I CALL Sophie later when Esme has fallen asleep. She is staying in the nearest Travelodge, 20 miles away.

'Soph, we need to leave. I can't put Es at risk anymore. Could you put us up, just for a while?'

'Of course,' she says. 'Stay as long as you need.'

I telephone Ben. He is at mine, waiting.

'Any sign?'

'Nothing,' he said. 'How is Es?'

'She's scared. She's tired. But at least she's here. I'm never letting her out of my sight again.

There is a pause on the line.

'I'm so sorry,' he says.

'What happens now? What do we do with him? We made our home with him, and he burned it down.'

'I know, Alice.' He pauses. 'You tried to tell me, and I didn't listen. You do nothing. You go and live your life. We'll figure something out.

He pauses and then adds, 'There's a missing piece, though. We haven't heard his story. What was he doing with her?'

'Nothing he could say could make me trust him ever again.'

'I understand. When are you home?'

'Tomorrow, they said.'

'I'll wait,' he says.

As I hang up, I already know that Ben won't change his life for his brother, and he won't put his children at risk for the same reason that I can't put Esme at risk. So why have I done it for so long? Why have I carried the burden on my own all this time? Why am I such a terrible mother, thinking that I can be everything to everyone, putting his needs above my daughter's?

I sit there in the white hospital, wondering what my options are, wondering if I can pack my things and run away with Esme. Who would look after Christopher though? What if he comes back and we aren't there?

But then I imagine me and Es in a flat, bright and small, with a new life, in a city, perhaps, and I wonder if there is any way we will ever get there.

BEN IS STILL THERE when we get back the next day. There has been no sign of Chris. Ben kneels down and looks at her, my small daughter.

'I'm so glad you're safe,' he says, his voice breaking.

AS I RUN a bath for her, later that night, I strip her down and turn her around in front of me, marvelling at her small shoulders, her tidy knee creases, her brown forearms. There isn't a scratch on her.

I didn't think he'd have hurt her, but that's just it, I didn't think he'd abduct her either. What did he want? What was he doing?

· · ·

'WHAT DID he do to you, Es?' I ask, a few days later. 'You can tell me. I won't be cross. Can you start at the beginning and tell me everything that happened?'

She looks at me suspiciously with her mousy eyes.

'Are you going to get cross with Christopher?' she asks.

I shake my head.

She shrugs and then continues.

'He just asked if I wanted to go for an adventure. He said you had said it was ok.'

'Where did you sleep?'

'In the hay,' she says.

'You must have been so cold, my darling.'

She nods.

'Were you scared?'

She nods.

'What did you eat?'

'He had some crisps.'

'Oh, darling,' I say, pulling her into a hug. 'What a fool I am, Es, to put you in such danger. He doesn't know what he's doing. But we can't live here anymore. We'll go to stay at Sophie's for a while.'

'What about school?'

'Don't worry about school.'

45

———

CHRISTOPHER

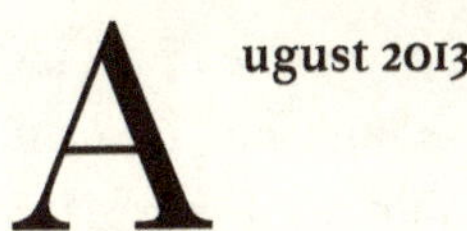

August 2013

WHAT DO I DO NOW? I whisper to the hedgerows the holders of the edges of things I can't stop here I can never go back I can never say sorry I hide in a ditch, and her voice crackles in and out like radio static she is angry angrier than she's ever been these days she's getting worse and worse, hungrier and hungrier and I don't know what more I can give her I was so worried she would be cross with me and she is because I didn't do what she asked me to I pick myself up and run 'til I am spent and out of breath I run 'til I don't know the place no more I run 'til my lungs sting 'til my calves ache three farms over I slump against a hawthorne hedge like oversized roadkill and catch my breath for a minute - its spines press through my shirt and into my heavy flesh the pain cuts through and keeps me in the land of the living her shrill voice rattles around my brain looking for an escape route I lie back in the hedgerow with all the chatter the birds try to chirp above her but her voice is a deafening roar.

Nowhere to go no money to my name no wallet no phone can't go back can't say sorry what now? what now? keep asking myself.

I lie there by a hawthorn hedge belly to the ground hands over my ears I'm trying to think things through, but she won't stop talking.

The rain starts gently but then it comes like a flood it falls with such force that it bounces back from the hardened ground the rain snakes down my face until I can taste the sweat. I'm wet through and don't even try to resist there is nowhere to hide I pull off my boots and my socks I peel my checked shirt and jeans off my body I walk out into the middle of the field and let the heavy rain wash me clean when I am in amongst it the roar surrounds me like a cloak and drowns her out almost.

46

THE VILLAGE

August 2013

THE LIVING ONES speak their minds over and over, they can't stop speculating. They rankle our tarmac back with their wild theories.

'He would never hurt a fly. The girl's fine, isn't she?'

'It's always the quiet ones.'

'It was unnatural them living like that – he should have been in supported housing.'

'Of all the things we've seen, this was the saddest.'

'It's that girl, she's never lost her grip on him.'

'He's never been free of his parents, never had a mind of his own.'

'She's better off now that he's gone.'

'What was she thinking anyway, shacked up with him?'

'What'll he do now, wandering on his own? He'll not make it through winter.'

'He'll become an itinerant, a traveller; a scarecrow, neither man nor beast. He'll fall through the cracks. Just like Leo did.'

'Hardly spoke a word, did he?'

ALICE TRIED SO hard to hold him up, but it didn't work, no matter how steady she was, because long ago he had forgotten himself. And the voice which lay furled in his childhood self was crowded out by this other voice, the one that called to him incessantly, that became stronger than his own because he was too weak to stop her. He had tried to keep her out for so long. He had used the last of his strength, and now, she rushed in on him and filled him, completely.

We saw him stark naked in the field, rivulets of rain cleaning his goose-pimpled skin. We watched him put himself in noisy places, talk to himself and keep the hubbub about him just to try to hush her. We saw him utterly helpless against her tide.

47

ALICE

September 2013

I TAKE Es to Cambridge for a week, but we can't settle.

When we get back to the village, we look for clues – dead animals, sticks in the road – but nothing is out of place. Es creeps around, unsure of herself in the space. We are quiet between ourselves.

In the days after it happened, the police set a dog to follow his scent, but the trail went cold at the corner of the road. Did he jump in the dyke to drown his scent? Did he just keep walking and walking, I wonder, until someone took him in? Did he hitch a lift with someone? I walk the streets with Esme. When my gaze is lifted, looking over the fields, I scan them for his form, for a figure running clumsily as he did, his lumbering hulk falling forwards over the furrows, and when my eyes look down to the ground, I can't help but look for clues, anything, no matter how small or insignificant.

I am always looking for him. I keep expecting him to burst in through the back door with some new tale or drama. I imagine the sound of his voice ringing up through the floorboards:

'Alice, are you there?'

When I am sitting in my armchair in the lounge, I can feel his presence behind me, but, when I turn, there is no one there.

It's the nights that are the worst. Whenever I scooch down under the covers, the smell of fresh sheets around me, I imagine his boots, the ones that he never used to lace up, his jeans, stained with layers of mud upon mud, his waxed jacket and his broad shoulders. I lie there and think of him, his big old body, him throwing it around as if he were a young boy. I imagine him cold and alone.

I shudder, but what can I do for him now? If he came to the door, I'd hate him, but at least I'd know he was safe.

I wonder if it haunts Ben like this too, and if he feels responsible like I do?

I don't know what to think, I don't know where to start looking for him. The places where he used to go are gone. I can't think that he'd even try to get to Ben's on his own. So, I don't know what to imagine for him.

48

CHRISTOPHER

September 2013

THE BLACK EARTH crumples like a pillow under me. Damp clods jut into my back, and I feel the wetness seep through my shirt and jumper to the skin. I must stink like a shit heap. The air gets into me wherever I sleep – hedgerow or barn – and I feel it all around me, like the pain that I deserve. Sandpaper skin and itchy scalp from not washing. I know I stink; I can feel the hum about me. Keeps folks away though, doesn't it? They'll not come near me if I stink of shit, of sweat, of unlove. My body's an ogre, falling over the fields. Ain't seen another human in days, only a matchstick man a field over, no one close, no one's eyes, ain't seen myself even, I'm just running.

Got to get out of these Fens, though. Got to keep walking. There's no preservation against the elements, like. Nothing to keep me molly-coddled against the wind. No fence, no bridge. I wanted to be out in it since they took the roof off Mum and Dad's house. It felt better that way, and I would have lived there then, except they put up the tape, and kicked me out. I don't want no house now though; don't know what I want. I want to be warm though. Out of this wind. 'Spose the cold helps sometimes though; it numbs me, numbs all the pain out, it gets things straight, gives me clarity. That's what I need, to get things straight again.

Where am I going, I ask the birds and the clouds, and I wonder if this is how Leo lived. When I get there, wherever it is that I am going, I ask myself where now? If he could do it, so can I. I look for a sign, an arrow in a cloud or on a pavement, the name of a town that I like, any little thing, and it guides me that way, see. Leo taught me that no one needs things. All you need is the clothes on your back. Perhaps I can be a wandering man, like Leo. I want to roam. But I want to have it figured out first, that's the main thing.

These past few days, something is different.

I'm a radio detuning, struggling to pick up her wavelength now. The more I walk, the fainter she becomes, as if I've left her behind me, as if she was only ever in the village, not in my head, like everybody said. The more I walk, the more I am stamping all that was wrong out of my body. All those things they said about me: retarded, broken, traumatised, schizophrenic, delusional. Stamping them down, like.

Nothing in my head now but the echo of my own voice, the feel of my tongue in my mouth. The further I walk, the more I am myself. My clothes get looser, my calves get tighter. I lie there when I wake, taking in the sweet sound that I haven't heard in years; silence. Feels I'm coming to clarity, somehow. I can hear myself.

I start to notice the pylons. These giants, straddling the lowlands, hold their bunched fists of wires. They stretch ahead for miles and miles. And like a punch in the heart – I just know it – they will take me where I need to go. It's like an epiphany; the land telling me so.

I walk and walk, my legs burning. Can't stop until I get there. I sleep in hedgerows and barns, anywhere that's dry and under a bit of cover. My whole body aches. I think of Leo, his sinewy old body baked brown and stripped bare. When you're always on the road like this, the fat burns away, and just the machine remains, the slow cogs turning, the miracle heart, buried under flesh and bone.

I forgot my Zyprexa; weren't no time to get it. Didn't think I wouldn't be coming back. Don't know what I thought I was doing that morning. Didn't do it though, managed to get away. I stood up to her, finally.

The doctor gave me pills to dull the voice. Her voice. My calves ache and my heart beats faster but I am done with it. The pills don't work anyway; they never have.

It was always about numbing me. Numbing me right down, sanding off the edges, 'til I still heard her voice all the time, dawn 'til dusk, but it just didn't bother me so much. It was like she melted right down into my brain and became a part of me, and I didn't even bother to try to get rid of her no more. It became like lying in the shallowest water and her washing over me and over me like a gentle tide. Over me, in through my mouth, all around my brain. She was everywhere.

49

———

ALICE

N ovember 2013

IT'S NOVEMBER NOW, and every single morning that I wake I think he wouldn't have survived if he was out in that.

He never quite became himself, was pulled back, always, by that girl, that girl, that girl. She was his world, and every-thing circled around her, even though she'd been gone forever. When she went, his world caved in.

If only there was a reset button. If only we could start again. If only he could have been dealt a fairer hand.

It wasn't her fault, it wasn't his either, but what do you do when your life starts off like that? How do you get to the source of it? How do you stop the black hole from dragging you and everything else that you hold dear into its vortex?

His body is so big and brutal. He doesn't care for it; he leaves his skin open to the elements, his shirt untucked, his boots untied and loose around his ankles. It makes me shudder, the thought of him out there on his own. The thought of his cold, unloved self. He had no sense of looking after himself, but his mother was a kind woman and his father too, no doubt, so I don't know where it came from.

Cassie, I should imagine.

I'm haunted by that cry of mine, the one I hurled out across the field. 'Christopher! Don't you ever come near my daughter again!'

I knew he was nearby; I could feel him. He would have heard me, and my body cranes with guilt at the thought of it. Even after what he did. Even still, even still.

My anger has slowed to a small, persistent burn. I'm angry at him but I don't want him to die. I don't know what to think. I don't know where to start looking for him because the places where he used to go are gone. I can't think that he'd even try to get to Ben's on his own. So, I don't know what to imagine for him.

Es won't let it go. She asks me over and over, 'Is he lost?' She draws pictures of him walking, hiding, running.

I pretend it is all okay for her. 'Who knows where he has gone, but I am sure he is safe and warm. He must be with friends, in a new village somewhere.'

'But he can't make friends, Mum, he's too strange.'

And what she says hangs in the air because we both know it's true.

Sometimes I don't know how to answer her questions.

'Is he coming back, Mum?'

'I don't know, love.'

'Is he missing too, now? Like he said Cassie was?'

50

─────

CHRISTOPHER

November 2013

To start with, I didn't know where I was going. But now I know. Figured it out as I walked along. I'm going to get Ben.

For so long, they've kept me there, in that walled-in village but I've got legs, ain't I? I'll walk my way around. I've got a voice, ain't I? I'll talk my way through it.

Miracle man. Living on the earth before I return to it, before the worms come and take me back. I've got years, I've got years left before I go. Maybe even forever.

That's why I'm going to go and get Ben. I mean where else would I go? He's all I've got.

But there's a reason I don't want to go, and it pokes at my heart, and that's that he's the last chance. If he says no, then I've got nowhere else to turn.

Feels strange, walking all this way without her, without

Cass. She's gone all quiet. We've always done everything together.

It's just me now.

Christopher.

51

CHRISTOPHER

November 2013

THE PYLONS SHOW me the way; they carry me with their strides across the land. I walk under them towards the setting sun.

I'm becoming a different animal now. Leaner, sharper. Like a fox. Like Leo.

You have to, to survive. Forget the former things, do not dwell on the past. This is the way now. One step and then another.

Ben will know what to do. He can't turn me away.

As I've walked, the things Leo told me have come back to mind: the things he'd eat from the hedgerows, things out of bins. Didn't plan it, didn't think it through. I'd have been too scared otherwise. Just had my old donkey jacket, the shoes on my feet, the clothes on my back. But now I'm here, halfway to somewhere and there's no turning back. I can do it. I can stay alive. Just you see if I don't.

At the beginning, I slept anywhere there was a hedgerow, a bit of shelter, I rolled in and tucked myself up to its spiny branches, tucked my chin down into my chest and fell into slumber. As it got colder and meaner, as the rain lashed at me, I thought it'd get harder, but you'd be surprised that you don't need the warm to sleep, that the body will succumb eventually anyway.

All you got to do is keep going. You'd be surprised what you can find in bins, service stations, out the back of restaurants. I never found any foodbanks, didn't really go into towns, but stuck to the main arteries; the motorways, the grand master pylons striding the land.

And one day there are signs I've seen before: his town, a street that I've been to before, just one time.

And then one day, it is broad daylight and I'm sneaking around in the woodland behind their house. I'll wait until the coast is clear. Wait and watch.

52

———

CHRISTOPHER

November 2013

I LIE THERE, up against his neat panel fencing. Garden all tidy like they are these days. I press my body up to the fence. I swear there is someone in the garden. 'Ben,' I whisper, 'there is so much I have to tell you.'

Can hear a windchime tinkling and the leaves of the willow. All I want is to be ok. To be a good brother, to explain it all.

I'm so tired. I came all this way to find him. I lie there at the fence, pressing my body to it, willing myself the courage to stand up and knock on his door. Say, 'Ben, I've missed you so much,' but I look down and my shoes have come undone at the ends. My clothes hang off me now, and I have the stench of death about me.

And then I hear him in the garden talking to Lucie. It sounds like they have a dog, and I just can't bring myself to say hello, to undo everything again. They seem happy enough. He is bright. This is his life now. What right have I to go banging on his door, dragging them all down again? I bite the tears down.

Better that I come when I'm better, all fixed. Good as new – how he'd want me to be.

After everything, all the walking, my heart slows and slows. I'm tired. I've come a long way. But he won't want to see me like this. I'll wait here a while, listening, and when I'm fixed, I'll go again.

I fall asleep there, pressed up against the panel. There's a bed of leaves and a scrap of tarp that I found in a farmer's field. Things could be worse.

At first light, the rain comes, and I pick up my tarp, pack it away in my bag and set out.

Walking is easy compared to everything else I've ever done. The road asks no questions. Asks nothing of me except that I carry on.

53

———

ALICE

 ugust 2014

IT'S BEEN A YEAR. A whole year.

How can he have vanished without a trace? How can I leave when he might come back looking for me? How can I live if I don't know if he's alive?

Es is eight now. Sassy and smart. Growing up with a hole in her heart.

This is what I wanted; I sometimes have to remind myself. For so long, I dreamed of this; a quiet house, just me and my girl.

It is just for us now, the house. The cool chequerboard floor where the light pours in and my wooden studio. No interruptions, just how we wanted.

But the thing is that, without Christopher, there's no heart. We don't love the place anymore.

'Should we move, Es?' I sometimes say, 'Would you like

to go somewhere new?' and we talk about it. But we always come back to the fact that this is where he'd look for us, if he ever did come home. And it wasn't so bad, was it?

We both know we'll never leave. The thing that held us here is gone, but still, we can't leave.

What are we supposed to do now? How are we supposed to live? I can't stop wondering if he's dead or alive. I wake with the image of his face each morning. They haven't found a body, but then, who is helping him to live? He wouldn't manage on his own. And there are these loose ends, that will stay with us forever now, these questions that hang over us each day. There is nothing so painful as a missing person, no explanation, just a mountain of unanswered questions that we face each day. The void wakes us up and stares at us over breakfast, follows us if we go for a walk and pokes at us if we feel the sun on our faces. And I can't see a way for us to get around it.

It was me that did it, that snapped the cord that bound us, that set him loose, spinning into the ether, all on his own, and now I won't leave this place. I can't leave; it ties you in, you see.

And so, we live quietly, hardly leaving the village, often watching at the windows, in case he should ever come home.

54

———

ES

T EN YEARS LATER:

December 2023

I am scrolling Instagram when I see the listing. It just happens to catch my eye. 'The Thing I Never Told Anyone.'

I am lying on the sofa, my legs hanging over the arm. It's Saturday. I've been out for coffee and a pastry. A little routine I've made for myself, since moving down to London for uni. Makes me feel looked after.

The thumbnail image for the exhibition is of a painting called *Missing Person* by a Christopher Bird. I sit up. A prickle runs down my spine.

The image is a portrait, but the face has been smudged away. I google Christopher Bird and find a minimalist website; no photo, no bio. Just these paintings of the Fens, blank and haunting. It could be him.

The show opens that night. I WhatsApp Mia and Stu, my course buddies.

'Hi, guys. A new exhibition tonight at the Portrait. Fancy it?'

They are always up for something free to do, and the pings come back straight away.

I love how London has become our gigantic playground. The Christmas lights are up, and it feels like it is always daytime in the city. I love it here.

We stop for a drink at the Chandos first, and I try to push the butterflies down with two pints of cider. I don't tell them why we're really here. But I feel sick as we approach the door. I'm glad I didn't come alone.

I push open the double-height door, and we step out of the pouring rain and into the bright room.

55

CHRISTOPHER

December 2023

I AM STANDING THERE FEELING like a fraud in a bad suit but Suzie from the gallery said I must come, I must come. I feel like an overblown fool; so out of place and yet, at the same time, my God, I can't believe my good fortune.

Vinny entered my work without telling me. The gallery emailed back months later telling me that I'd won the chance to exhibit, and they'd like to meet me. But by then, Vinny was sick, so Liam came with me on the train, and I clutched my canvases to my chest.

Two months later, and it has all come together but tonight, I came alone.

Suzie, the curator, is small in her green trouser suit, as bubbly as a glass of champagne, overflowing with laughter about this or that. She's kind to me; she treats me nice but don't treat me as special. I don't know what to make of it all, really.

I'm standing there in my suit, itchy on the neck, sipping white wine, and I watch the front door of the gallery. It's a long thin room and the doors at the far end have panes of glass the whole way up encased in steel. Tall, heavy doors. Outside it is dark and there is a constant stream of traffic and rain. The rain still falls in the city, but it's different here. It just bounces off people. No one seems weighed down by it.

And then in walks a girl with strawberry blonde hair.

56

ES

December 2023

It's him. I know it is as soon as I see him.

He is standing there looking as awkward as fuck, in a suit that he looks repulsed by.

Christopher.

He is slightly overweight, and his hair looks like a choir boy's haircut with the fringe cut straight across. He clasps his hands together in front of him while his eyes flit around the room. He looks nervous and out of place. His cheeks are red like they always were. I can't believe he's alive, and at the same time, I'm so glad he had it in him. Fuck. How did he do it?

'My God, it's him,' I say.

I walk straight up to him and shake his hand.

I look him in the eyes and see a flash of recognition and then he doubts himself.

He flinches, and a shadow of regret passes over his face for the briefest of moments. He looks scared.

'Christopher,' I say, as I shake his hand, and he looks into my eyes.

He seems confused.

The emotions wash over his face like watercolours, like light gels in a darkened room: timid, uncertain, disbelieving.

He could never hide the way he really felt, and it makes me burst into a grin despite myself.

'Es?' he asks.

I nod, blinking back a tear.

'Yes. It's me,' I say, feeling giddy with the surge of questions that flood my brain. I fling my arms around his body.

57

ES

D ecember 2023

'MUM, can you come down? I'm really struggling with my course, and I've got the flu, and I just miss you,' I lie.

'You miss me?' she says incredulously. 'What time is it?'

'It's late. I'm sorry. I just had to call you. Everything is getting on top of me.'

She is silent for a minute on the other end of the call. She is surprised, I can tell. She is probably wondering if there is something else behind it, which of course there is.

'Sorry you're feeling rough, love,' she says. 'I'm at Dungeness at the moment – you'd love it – so bleak.'

I am uninterested in her midlife crisis road trip just now. We are still learning this new way of being mother and daughter now that we live apart. She's gone mad and given everything up for that van, to travel around the UK looking into bleak seas. Finding herself, apparently.

'I'll be there in a few weeks, anyway, picking you up for Christmas.'

I shake my head.

'No, Mum, you don't understand, I really need you to come now.'

For so long, it was just me and her. Forever and ever, it seemed. And life was so quiet. Especially after he went. She wanted to keep it normal for me while I did all my growing up, but what the hell was normal about having no father and then the only half-father figure that you had, running away?

'I could come up tomorrow afternoon. But there's no room for me is there? I could stay in the van?'

'I guess you could sleep on the floor?'

I only moved in a month ago, but Jess is cool. She won't mind. I needed something low-key after a few weeks in the hellhole that was halls in Southeast London. Sweaty, high-rise prisons with no communal areas made my first few weeks awful, but this was much better, and I felt like I was finding my feet. I had my course buddies; I had my little armour against the world. But I'm not totally myself around Jess, yet, and I wonder how she'd really feel about my Mum gatecrashing our tiny flat.

'Err yeah, that's fine,' she says. 'Es. Is everything ok?'

'Well, like I said, I'm feeling really ropey, and I could really use being looked after or at least being with someone, you know? And since you've got renters, it's not like I can come home.'

She sighs.

'Es, I had to. I couldn't stay there. We'd had enough of it, hadn't we? What more could it have given us? This is so much better, travelling around in the van, no one to wait for. Just getting on with things.'

There he is, still hovering at the edges of our conversations, ten years on. And although I didn't really want to be molly-coddled, it was slightly disconcerting that Mum was able to snip the thread that held us. She'd completely changed. Gone off the rails, fallen in love with herself and her van.

I guess it's only fair that she lives a little, and it's better than the alternative – her mum calling up all the time, making her feel guilty for living a life like her mum's mum had done to her.

Mum had sold everything, just like Leo. Only she made the van her home, not the road.

'Mum, another thing. When you get here, can we go straight into town? There's something I need to show you.'

'Um, yeah, of course. I thought you were feeling ill though?'

'Yeah, I am, but it's really important.'

'Ok, sure, see you tomorrow, babe.'

'Come as soon as you can.'

58

———

ALICE

December 2023

Es TELLS me we are going to see an exhibition. What a strange thing for your grown-up daughter to want to do if they feel sick.

I pull up outside hers, after battling Friday night traffic for over an hour and she practically drags me onto the train, no time to even have a wee before we are swaying on our way to the bustling heart of the city. I have been driving Mollie, the camper van, around the coast. I left when Es did – I couldn't bear to be left alone – and I'd only been gone two months, but I was feeling better than I had in years.

'Darling, what's going on?'

I look at her, all emo with her pink fringe and DMs. She is beautiful in her own way, and she knows it.

'You seem ok, hon, you don't have a temp.'

'Yeah, I'm just struggling with the course and all, Mum. We'll talk about it later.'

She drags me to the National Portrait Gallery, and walks straight in.

Takes my hand at the doorway and I can feel that she is trembling.

'What is it?' I say, turning to look at her.

'Mum' she says, holding my forearms with an urgency, and staring straight into my eyes. 'I found him.'

I turn and look.

Christopher.

59

—————

ES

D ecember 2023

MUM JUST STARES AT HIM, her mouth fallen open.

She walks up to him, blinded by tears. She reaches for his face and holds it in her hands.

'Christopher,' she says. 'You're alive.'

'Alice,' he says. 'Alice,' and then looking between us, he says, 'I love you two more than anything I've ever loved.'

'How?' Mum says. 'How did you survive?'

'I walked. And as I walked, I got better. The voices stopped. I'm okay now. The walking made me better.'

Mum cries as if it's the best news anyone could have given her, as if it's the best answer to the question she's been asking for ten years.

'How long are you here?' she asks, 'Can we talk? I want to know everything. I thought you were dead.'

The anger has melted away in five minutes. She loves him.

'I'm meant to stay until nine, but shall we go for food afterwards?'

And she finds herself nodding, at this man who disappeared from our lives and has somehow become someone else entirely.

MUM and I walk slowly around the exhibition, taking in the images. They are portraits of secrets and the way they change our lives. Fucking tell me about it.

'I just can't believe it. He's alive.'

She keeps looking over her shoulder to check if he's still there.

There is the big canvas with the face smudged away, the one I saw in the paper. It looks like a photograph in a bleached-out room, but I look closer, and it is a painting. Is it him? I stand close and take in the brush strokes, the blue-white light. I wonder why he doesn't have a face. I look for a description of the piece but a note on the wall just says, 'I did the worst thing I could to the ones I loved the most in the world.'

My heart clenches. I know it is us. The past tense. Loved.

'Mum,' I say, clutching her arm. 'Don't forget what he did.'

She nods and takes my hand. Her forearm is trembling.

LATER, we go to a noodle bar and sit there in a steamed-up window by the sizzling kitchen. The rain streams down the windowpanes. It is odd to be so close to him. I want to touch his face too, to check he's real. He looks different. His hair is cut closer to his head and his face is thicker set. He's put on weight. It's been ten years since we saw him. We can't stop looking at him, noticing all the ways his face has changed.

'It's been so long. I can't believe you're alive. How did you live?' Mum asks him, and we listen.

'Well, I walked. After the barn, I knew I could never come back. All I wanted was to come back, but I couldn't get to you. I couldn't tell you what I was doing.'

'What were you doing?'

I'm surprised she's not screaming at him.

'I'll tell you. The voice was getting stronger and stronger. Her voice. Cassie. She was saying over and over again, "Kill her and I'll never leave you. She is taking you away from me. Get rid of her and I'll never go!" She was saying it over and over again, I felt like I was going crazy.'

He puts his head in his hands.

Mum and I share a look.

'I'm so sorry, Es,' he says and puts a hand out to mine. 'I didn't understand why she was saying it, she was such a sweet girl. I couldn't, I could never have hurt you, Esme, but you don't understand what it was like. I told her that I couldn't and do you know what she said? She said "There are roads and cars that will do the job for you. All it would take is a shove. No one would know except for me and you."'

I pull my hand away.

'I'm so sorry, Es, but she kept saying it over and over. I trusted her, I always would, I loved her dearly, but I knew something wasn't right.

'It was when we were walking, and she said "Now! Push her now," and that's when I knew something was wrong.

'Es, I could never have hurt you. She was telling me to, but I could never have. I loved you. I took you to that barn to keep you out of harm's way, to get you away from her voice. You know that, don't you?'

And Mum and I are quiet because we didn't know.

'You ran away with Es to protect her?' Mum says, her chin wobbling.

He nods.

'But I couldn't tell you because you thought I had done the worst thing and, after it all, I thought it was best to disappear. I knew you wouldn't believe me.'

And I can feel the calamity of it all shaking my body; the guilt, the unanswered questions, the breaking of all that we had built together.

I feel like my body has been slammed into a wall.

Later that night, after setting Mum up in the lounge on a makeshift bed of sofa cushions and spare sheets, I go to my bedroom and close the door behind me. I turn to the window where the leaves of the lime tree flicker golden in the glow of the streetlight.

Is it true? For all these years, I have pretended that I wasn't scared, so Mum could believe she had saved me from that monster Christopher.

But now, I slide my back down the door until I am collapsed in a heap on the beige carpet. Even before I reach the floor, the tears spill over, and I am that seven-year-old again, my small hand consumed in Christopher's.

In my tiny two-bedroom flat, I sit staring at my face in the wardrobe mirror.

He tried to kill me. He tried to save me.

I have never known which one is true.

60

THE VILLAGE

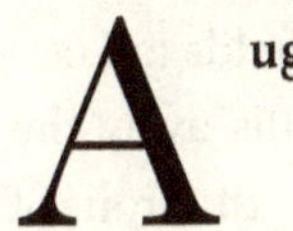

ugust 2013

'COME ON, ES, LET'S GO' Christopher says.

He walks with Esme through the quiet lanes, and the smell of cut hay is in the air. Butterflies cross their path. It is early morning but already warm.

He walks faster than she can manage, so she runs alongside him to keep up. He pulls her arm with determination. He pulls her so her feet don't rest on the ground, they just skim it.

Later, she walks ahead of him, and he notices the fuzz of her hair, pulled back into bunches and her nut-brown shoulders.

She thinks it is all a great adventure.

His palms tingle with sweat as the adrenaline pumps around his body. A cacophony of voices has made its home in his mind.

A lorry approaches, and the voice says, 'NOW.'

He stretches out his hand to her shoulder and is about to shove her sideways with all his weight, when she turns her head, smiles at him and sees his hand ready to push.

He drops his hand to his side and the enormity of what he has almost done drowns him.

'No, no, no, no,' he says, and he takes her hand and starts to run with her. They cut across the fields at World's End Lane.

'Where are we going, Chris?' Esme asks in her small voice.

'Don't worry, you'll like it,' he says, and she follows him, trusting implicitly.

He runs faster now. He takes her across the fields to Leo's greenhouse, which is overgrown, but Chris pulls away the long grasses and there it all is; his shears, the roll of bedding. Just as it was before. Nature has sown its green grass over everything, and it is all being slowly swallowed again by nature.

'I ain't been back here in years,' Christopher says.

'Who lived here?' Esme asks.

'My friend Leo.'

'You'll be safe here.'

They sit down, and Christopher sets about releasing things from the grip of the grass.

After a while, Esme fidgets and frowns.

'I want to go home. I'm cold.'

CHRIS GETS MORE AGITATED, and he starts mumbling. He paces up and down, chewing his fingers. He starts whispering to himself.

'I believe that Cassie wants the best, truly truly I do. So, I should listen to her, shouldn't I, Mum? She'll keep me safe; I know she will. She's not bad is she, Cass, she's my best friend. Even though she went away, best friends never change. Thicker than blood we are. Best friends 'til the end of the earth. So, if she tells me to do something, I've got to do it, haven't I? That's right, isn't it, Mum? That's what friends are for. Who cares what the voices say if she is the one saying it? Who cares what they say if it keeps me close to her?'

AND THEN HE starts shouting at someone else, talking to them like they are right here with us. Es shrinks back into her corner.

'Let's go home, Chris,' Es says.

'She won't come if we don't stay. Got to stay or she won't know where to go, will she?'

'Who is Cassie? Why do you talk about her all the time? Did you love her?'

Christopher nods. 'You're Cassie too though, I mean, you're just like Cassie. I do love her; I'll always love her. She's my best friend.'

Esme shakes her head. 'I'm Esme. I've always been Esme!'

Christopher laughs.

'No, no, you used to be Cassie, I'm sure of it, in a different lifetime perhaps. Have you found a way back to me after all? I've been looking for you all this time.'

'I don't know,' Esme whimpers, looking down.

Chris grabs her by the arms again and pulls her jaw up to look him close in the face.

'Tell me that you're her, and then everything will make sense. You have come back to me after all this time.'

Esme starts crying and there is no one to hear her.

'I'm just me. I want to go home,' Esme says through her tears to Christopher. 'I want Mummy.'

She tries to pull open the door on its runner and it jars.

'Christopher! Let me out!'

He shakes his head.

'We have to wait for her, she's coming. She's here, she's in my head. We need to hide.'

'Christopher, you're not making any sense. I want Mummy,' Esme whimpers.

'No. We'll go somewhere else,' he says, 'it's not safe here.'

Esme has no choice but to trust him.

He takes her two fields over, where they find a barn with its back to the road and the corrugated iron panels peeling away. Inside, there is an old red tractor, some hay bales stacked up in one half, and stacks of ploughs and farm machinery tangled up in the other.

Esme wonders whether she should run, but she isn't sure of the way. She had better stay with Christopher. She isn't sure that he's ok. He is acting strange, and she knows he has these breakdowns sometimes. Mummy has told her. She isn't sure how she is meant to make him better, but she can stay with him, that she can do. He pulls two crushed packets of crisps from his pocket.

'There you go.'

She nibbles them quietly. She doesn't want to talk. Christopher seems different.

Esme whimpers and cries through the night, chewing bits of straw from the hay bales. She licks the corrugated iron in the morning, the dew filling her belly with its cool metallic tang. Chris needs to eat too. He chews his fingers as he realises it's over. He's done it this time; he's gone too far. No way back.

And then, in the evening, Es hears a dog barking far off, and she prays that someone is coming to find them because she needs Mummy and she is so cold. Someone needs to come to make Christopher better. They need a grown-up who knows what to do.

Christopher is dozing but the dogs snap him out of his reverie.

He wakes and backs away from her.

'I have to go,' he says. 'They are coming. I have to go. You be safe now, little one.'

And at the same time, the officers are running across the field to her.

She looks towards the door, where a dog is sniffing and scratching outside. They force the door down, and there they are: two police officers and two dogs. She looks back and Christopher has gone.

There is a lump in her throat. She wants them to rescue Christopher, too. He needs to be rescued just as much as she does, but the lump is too big, and it shuts her words back up inside her mouth because she doesn't know if they are the right ones or not. She doesn't want to get him into trouble, so she lets him disappear.

61

ES

December 2023

THE NEXT MORNING, we text Christopher and ask him to meet us at a Turkish cafe that serves brunch.

'Will you be able to find the way?' Mum texts, and I have to remind her that I think he's different now.

We sit on a low seat in the window. I order mint tea while Christopher and Mum look at each other. It's like they are stumbling over the ten years' worth of words they'd like to say.

Mum keeps saying, 'You're like a different person. How did you live?'

She has asked him that so many times. And he tells us about the walking, and how the more he walked, the more he found himself.

'Why didn't you tell us you were alive?'

He shrugs in that self-effacing way, and Mum nearly bursts with rage.

'Don't you know we were waiting for you?' she says, looking at him, watching his reaction. 'For ten years we've been waiting', she adds in a whisper.

I watch her talking, spitting the words out, and there are tears with them all. Rage and love are all mixed up. She has never loved anyone as much as him.

'I thought you were better off without me. I thought you could never forgive me,' he mumbles.

'Don't you know what it cost me?' she rails. 'I spent my life on you. I gave up my life for you! And then you tried to tear the very heart out of my life, and then you vanished, and then I spent years waiting for you. Fuck, it makes me so angry.'

She is trembling with rage. I pour her a glass of coffee and she piles in two sugars.

'I tried so hard to fix you, Christopher. I tried everything I could. And there was a whole person in you that I never saw.'

'You couldn't fix me, Al, nobody could. I had to get out of the village, that's all.'

'Does Ben know?'

He shakes his head.

'Are you going to tell him? He's going to go out of his mind.'

He shrugs and takes a drink. There is a spread of steaming flatbreads, dried fruit, yoghurt and spicy sausage.

'I went there, I walked all the way to his, if you can believe that. I lay there against his fencing, all new and straight. I heard him in the garden with Lucie. But then I was too ashamed, and I kept walking. Only then I didn't know where I was going.'

'I swear I'm telling him today if you don't.'

He nods and holds up his hands.

'Tell us what you did, Chris.'

And he starts talking, threading together that life and this.

'I walked and walked. After Ben's, I ended up in Birmingham where they asked me how I was going to get through the winter. They gave me a tent, a fleece, a sleeping bag, water, hot soup. They wanted nothing in return. There are many reasons people are on the streets, they said. I stayed in the shadows, ready to pounce if they came too close. Wasn't used to people anymore, so I kept myself to myself. But all the roads went to London, so I ended up being dragged there, too.

'Then, eventually, I got to Whitstable, a seasidey place. Liked it. There was a hostel that would have me, so I made a home for myself. Started painting again. Bloke I got to know, Vinny, from the centre, he helped me along a little. Got me set up with some canvases and some paints, said, "Show me what you can do," then stood back with a smirk on his face. Didn't think I had it in me. But it's all in me,' he said, tapping his nose. 'Al, you know that? Couldn't speak when he saw my picture. You taught me.

So, then I went out on the street and talked to people and painted them. I asked them, "What's your biggest secret? What's the thing you've told no one?' And I got some juicy ones. And because I was the secret bearer, I was allowed to tell it in my own way, with my paints, but it had to be hidden, too. I still go out on the streets; it unpicks me like wool to let all those little secrets go into the world. It's my favourite thing. They whisper things like, "I don't love my husband anymore," or "I think my dad is cheating on my mum," and I tell them out loud in colour. The burden is gone then, see. I take it from them.

'But then Vinny got sick, he got cancer. The doctors zapped him, and his body couldn't take it. He died this year. But he'd left me a secret. Entered me for this art show, took pictures of my paintings, sent them off and I won. I won this award to come and show my work in London. Here. I'm only at the beginning, you see. He'd be proud of me, mind, Vinny would.

So, I walked it all away from me, and then I took peoples bad feelings too, tied them all up in paint, took them away.

One thing Vinny said though, he said, "The thing with a secret, Chris, is that it can eat you alive," so I've got to tell you, I've got to tell you my secret right now before it eats me anymore.'

'What is it?' Mum asks.

'I dared Cassie to run. It was my fault she died that day.'

62

ALICE

December 2023

FOR THE FIRST time in my life, I have closure. All the doors have softly closed, and I can drive away from London with no guilt.

Es is quiet this morning when I leave, but she's just a bit under the weather, I think. Winter is closing in; she has her end-of-year exam.

I am heading back to Dungeness for two weeks until Christmas when I'll come back to London, to be with her.

When she moved out, that was it, home had gone. The idea of it. We were scattered like leaves, and I knew I had to go, I'd been waiting so long. Who'd have thought in all the world that she'd find him again, like that, in London, of all places?

I still own the house in the village, but it doesn't call to me now, I think I'm done with it. I've got tenants. I might sell it but I wanted to keep it open just in case I ever wanted to go back there.

AFTER CHRISTMAS, in the cold and quiet of January, I think of Chris. I look up his website on my phone, sitting at a beach in Poole. He gave me his card, wary about being like he used to be, overly needy. He said to email if I wanted to.

And I held off for a month, but the thought of him, my friend, my closest one, echoes around the shell of myself, and I email him, just the one line:

SHOULD WE GO BACK?

63

———

CHRISTOPHER

M arch 2024

WE ARRANGE to meet there in March. I catch three different buses to get there, feeling sicker the closer I get.

The sun is pressing through today though and the daffodils are peeking up through the soil. I take a deep breath. I can do this. Butterflies tumble in my chest, like a thrumming inside of me.

I stand in the village of my past, across the road from where my house used to be. And I remember it all, like a roar of engines, like a rush of blood.

'I'M GOING to get a packet of Rolos,' I shout and run right across the road without looking to the left or the right.

'What are you going to get, Cassie?' I call from the other side, spinning around.

'Dairy Milk! My favourite!'

She hesitates at the kerb. The number 19 bus is coming.

'Come on!' I shout. 'Dare you!'

She steps off the kerb and begins to run. Her lace trips her up, and she falls onto the tarmac.

And then there is a bang.

I see it all.

Leo comes running, then someone else. There is a mother with her toddler, shielding her eyes. Someone runs for Cassie's parents; someone runs for the doctor.

A kind man from the bus gets off and tries to help but there is too much blood. It is everywhere, sticky and dark.

I run to her, hold her face in my hands and stare into her vacant eyes.

I CAME WILLINGLY TODAY. It feels like we have to tie it all up and lay it to rest somehow. We've all been on the run from this place for so long.

I find Alice and Esme at the crossroads near Mum and Dads, and we awkwardly hug. There is sadness there, in Alice's eyes; sadness for what is lost between us. We were never lovers, but friends. But so many years have gone now. Her eyes brim with tears even now, because we can't get it back, that life.

I would give anything to undo time.

We cross the road to Mum and Dad's place, a new-build on flat land now. They've filled in the ditch but left the same privet hedge along the front of the property. I reach out to touch a lime-green leaf, and it is as if I am touching the past, somehow.

We walk past the Five Bells: all gentrified, to the village shop, a Spar now. Cross the road where it happened.

Over to the graveyard, where I find her little stone:

Cassandra Mills

> *Gone too soon.*
> *1st February 1982 – 18th August 1989.*

I stop by Mum and Dad's graves, too. Wait by Cassie's the longest though. What would she be like today? What if she were here with me right now?

'Rest in peace, Cass,' I whisper, touching the moss-coloured stone.

Al and Es stop for a while at the graves of her mum and dad.

We walk along World's End Lane, past the farm buildings.

I take a deep breath. I'm free, even though the butterflies thrum. It's not under my skin no more; feels like I'm finally free. This place has had its claws in me for so long. I never knew I could walk away, not until I was pushed out of the nest. Not until I had no other choice.

I leave Al and Es at the corner and walk up through the field, to Leo's glasshouse. It's all smashed in now. A few bits of glass remain, and the grass has grown right through it all.

Still remember that night, talking in the dusk with Leo and Cass. The day before the world ended.

Remember that other morning, too, when Esme's little, panicked eyes looked at me like I was all she had in the world.

I make my way back to the road and then we loop back around to the start, the road leading out of the village, the way I ran, eleven years ago.

And here I am, still alive. Who would have thought it?

We walk past our house; mine, Alice and Esme's. The

place I belonged. Before it all went wrong. Before I broke things.

There's a new family there now. Two little kids and a puppy.

Seems like a different lifetime that I was there, painting in that top bedroom, trying to get away from all the noise. Strange how all these layers of life get laid down on top of each other, and you can't remember what it was like before, those old ways.

Things change one day, and then you can never get back to how it was before.

'It never stops, does it, Alice? Life, I mean,' I say, and she smiles and shakes her head.

'It never stops until it really stops.'

And I remember how it is an unbearable weight when life goes out like a candle that can never be relit. Once it's gone, it's gone.

For all the pain that I caused to Alice and Es, I think they still love me. I saw it in their eyes when we found each other again. Warily, but even so. I know because they had spent ten years searching for me.

We stand on a street corner after we have walked around the place. The sun is bright. It is a crisp day.

'So, what now?' Alice asks.

'Pub?'

'I meant in life.'

'Oh! I'll stay in Whitstable,' I say. 'I like it there, I've got friends, I've got the sea. I'll keep painting. You've got my email if you want to come to visit.'

Her eyes brim with tears and she pulls me into a hug.

'I'm so glad you're okay, Christopher. I'm so glad.'

'I'm going to keep driving Mollie around until we find a

place that feels like home. For the first time in my life, I am lost, but I quite like it,' she says.

Es says, 'I'm at uni for another two years. Fashion and journalism.'

'Can't believe you're grown now, Es,' I say, and I want to pat her on her head, but I daren't. I daren't look her fully in the eye, neither.

I don't want to worry her. I don't want her to think I am how I was before. I can't remember how I was before. It's like I have amnesia, like I was a different person now.

We stand there awkwardly for a minute or two, us three together like before, and then they turn and walk away to Mollie, the lemon-coloured van parked in the verge.

'You'll be okay, Chris?'

I nod. 'Yes, there'll be a bus along in a minute.'

And it feels sad in a way, but things have been wrapped up. I can put away this part of me, neatly folded.

I DON'T ASK for a lift; I don't want to overburden them like before. I don't know quite what they think of me now, after all this. If they think I'm still lost, or if they can see the new me, the one that was hiding for so long. Not hiding, actually; I think I hadn't quite been born. But I'm happy now. I've got my painting. I've got my friends at the supported housing. I've got the sea. It's a good place, light and full of sunshine.

I am not mad.

It is a thing I have come to learn over the years and am so grateful for. I am not mad. I just walked and walked until the clarity came. They were wrong, all the doctors. They were all wrong. I am not mad.

Alice and Esme both put their arms out of the windows

to wave as they pull away and then their van turns the corner and accelerates south towards the towns.

I wait for the next bus to take me to Peterborough, to London, to Whitstable. Back home. But just then, over the road, there is a rustling behind the privet at the top of Mum and Dad's drive. Where their house used to be, I should say.

I turn and she is there.

Her lean arms, the white embroidered top, her yellow shorts, the Alice band.

She is flesh and blood. She steps, she walks, she breathes.

She wears that same grin.

She has not aged, but she has been fixed, put together again.

'Chris!' she says as if she is surprised to see me.

My stomach drops to the floor.

I turn and retch into the verge.

My eyes are lying to me, and I don't understand why.

'Cassie?'

My mind reels.

All these years, walking away from her, forgetting her presence, learning that she wasn't real, that I had made her up, taking drugs to convince myself, talking therapy and the walking, all the walking.

And now she is here again.

I look over my shoulder, to where I just watched Alice and Es drive away.

'Alice,' I whisper, 'I don't know what to do.'

But she has gone.

My pulse is loud in my ears, my tongue is numb.

I cross the road and reach out to touch her arm, but she pulls away with a shrill cackle.

'Can't catch me!' she calls, and she darts back into the

embrace of the willow, the one remaining relic of the old garden. The willow leaves fall back into place behind her, hiding her from sight.

Everything in me wants to go after her, to touch her, to talk to her.

But it's someone else's lawn now, and I'm not about to go running around on their property; that would be madness.

And anyway, my feet won't move, and the bus comes along the road and stops dead at the bus stop, obscuring my view.

Enough. I take a deep breath.

I climb on board the bus and make my way up the aisle to sit on the back seat. I turn to see if I can see her out of the back window.

But I can't see her in the garden anymore; there is just the privet hedge, with its waxy, shining leaves and the willow fronds waving slowly in the breeze.

Perhaps it was a funny turn, I think. I am not mad, I remind myself.

Perhaps the emotions are all getting on top of me; it's been strange to see Alice and Esme again after so long.

Perhaps it's the heat.

I turn back to face the front; bus journeys already make me feel as sick as a dog without all the rest of it.

But just then a girl gets on, in a white top and yellow shorts, with an Alice band in her hair.

I smile in spite of myself. Cass.

Because I knew it in my heart, didn't I?

That in coming back here, I would leave the door open again to her.

That was why I came.

'I'll always look after you,' I whisper, as she walks towards me.

ACKNOWLEDGMENTS

Christopher, Running is a story that has been with me for many years. I started writing about the Fens in my English lessons at school, trying to get under the skin of the place. I wrote most of the book on my MA in 2006-2008. I had feedback suggesting that there wasn't really much of a plot, just a book in which things happened, so I hid the manuscript in a drawer for a few years. I have since taken the whole book apart and put it back together several times and now it is a book that I love.

So my first thanks go to the Fens, for giving me that sense of mystery and being the first thing I truly wanted to write about. I wrote because I couldn't understand it and it fascinated me. Thanks go to my Uncle John for being our favourite and making me and my siblings laugh. When you died, my siblings and I refused to believe it, and I think perhaps that sense of things hanging open, and remaining unfinished, is where this story was born.

Thanks to my parents for their unwavering support. Thanks to my children for taking my mind off writing with their endless string of requests. Thanks to all the memories laid down of big skies, open fields and polytunnels full of debris. Thanks to my Dad's folkloric tales that intrigued and always left me wondering.

Thanks to all the feedback I have had over the years on this manuscript. Huge thanks to Jordan Mulligan, who edited the manuscript with clarity and precision. Thanks also go to Mark Swan for that wonderful cover, full of menace, loneliness and the wild.

Thanks to my online writers group for all your advice and encouragement and my amazing beta readers who gave me such valuable feedback.

This book has been with me for more than half of my life and like a burden lifted, it is now set free. I hope that it speaks to you and gives you a flavour of those misty and secretive flatlands.

Elisabeth

If you enjoyed *Christopher, Running* please leave a review on Amazon or GoodReads. Every review will help another reader to find this book.

If you'd like to stay up to date with my writing news, sign up to my books mailing list here: https://preview.mailerlite.io/forms/1556505/159822437620385506/share

And if you like reading about the ups and downs of the creative life, sign up to my Substack newsletter here: https://substack.com/@minersbyelisabethpike

You can also find me here: elisabethpike.co.uk

And on socials @elisabethpikewriter (Instagram, Facebook and TikTok)

Lastly, if you enjoyed this, and would like to see more static caravans and epic journeys on foot, then you'll love *Murmuration*, a YA dystopian survival story, which was released in 2024 and shortlisted for the Kindle Storyteller Award!

Thanks so much for reading!